Astral Plane Publishing

Mourning Sun

The First Highland Home Novel

Shari Richardson

Astral Plane Publishing Books are published by

Astral Plane Publishing
120 Oak Road
York, PA 17402

Copyright © 2011 by Shari Richardson

All rights reserved. No part of this book may be reproduced in any form or by any means without the prior written consent of the Publisher, excepting brief quotes used in reviews.

All Astral Plane Publishing titles, imprints and distributed lines are available at special quantity discounts for bulk purchases for sales promotions, premiums, fund-raising, educational or institutional use.

Special book excerpts or customized printings can also be created to fit specific needs. For details, write the office of the Astral Plane Publishing Special Sales Manager, Astral Plane Publishing, 120 Oak Road, York, PA, 17402, Attn: Special Sales Department.

ISBN: **978-1460983263**

First Astral Plane Publishing Trade Paperback Printing: March 2011

Printed in the United States of America

Other Titles by Shari Richardson are available via Astral Plane Publishing

http://astralplanepublishing.blogspot.com/

About The Author

Shari Richardson holds a master's degree in English Education and has spent much of her life teaching students the joy of reading and writing. Her love of writing began when she was in elementary school and has carried through her entire adult life. Shari lives in Pennsylvania with her two Chihuahuas.

Table of Contents

Chapter 1..1
Chapter 2..22
Chapter 3..36
Chapter 4..47
Chapter 5..64
Chapter 6..75
Chapter 7..93
Chapter 8..108
Chapter 9..122
Chapter 10..128

Chapter 1

The young woman sat beside the bed, holding the boy's hand. Her lips moved in silent prayer, pausing only when he moved restlessly and moaned.

"Mathias?" Her voice was soft but rich.

He moaned again, but didn't wake. The young woman began to pray once again.

"Kathryn!" Mathias sat upright, searching the room with blind eyes. "Kathryn, run. Don't look back, just go!"

"Mathias, my love, I'm right here." She helped him lay back, smoothing her hand over his fevered brow. "Rest, my darling. You'll be well soon."

Mathias lay down, tossing restlessly. From time to time, he would whisper "Kathryn," before slipping farther into unconsciousness. Each time he spoke her name, Kathryn kissed Mathias and resumed her prayers.

Hours passed, but Kathryn, consumed by the life that drained from the man she loved, didn't notice the light draining from the day. She prayed. She held Mathias' hand. She soothed him when he was restless. Outside the window, the sun sank into the horizon. The sound of waves crashing against the shore slipped into the silence that now filled the room.

As the last of the light left the room, Kathryn rose to light a candle. When she returned to her place by his bedside, she set the candle on the table and leaned down to see Mathias better in the flickering light. She put her hand upon his chest and then sat by his side and lay her ear against his still chest.

"No," she whispered, curling her hand into a fist on his chest. "Oh Mathias, I can't live without you." Tears slipped down her cheeks as she closed her eyes and let the grief take her.

Mathias' eyes snapped open. Had she been watching, Kathryn would have seen that warm, dark eyes of his life were gone, replaced by pools of deepest, coldest black. He reached for Kathryn's hand where it lay on his chest, pulling it up to his lips.

"Mathias?" Kathryn blinked away her tears. Her eyes opened wide in disbelief, but there was no fear in her gaze, only the love she had for this beautiful boy.

Mathias licked his lips and ran his nose along the length of Kathryn's arm. She stayed frozen by his side, mesmerized by his gaze, which never flickered from her own. Even after his teeth sank easily into the warm flesh at the bend of her elbow, Kathryn never flinched. The room filled with a wet sucking, disrupted only by Kathryn's one brief gasp. Mathias lovingly cradled her arm against his lips as he drank, insensitive to the monstrosity of his act.

When Kathryn lay pale and still, Mathias blinked slowly. He looked down at the beautiful, pale and cold woman whose glassy eyes were riveted on his face. He brushed his hand along her cheek, lovingly caressing her face as he had done so often in life. It was only when she didn't smile and ask for his kiss that understanding slowly dawned in his gaze and he screamed.

"Kathryn, my love, my heart, my sun. What have I done?" His hands pulled at his face, drawing it into a gruesome mask of pain and anguish.

Lifting her body with infinite care, Mathias lay Kathryn on the bed from which he had so recently risen to this new and monstrous life. He closed her eyes and kissed her pale lips lovingly. "I will mourn you for eternity," he whispered before he threw himself out the window.

***

My eyes snapped open, my heart galloping along as though I'd just run a marathon. The last image of the young man's anguished face, hauntingly beautiful in his pain, lingered in my mind.

"Mairin, are you okay?" my mom called from the hall outside my bedroom.

"Yeah Mom," I said. "Just a weird dream."

Mom stepped into my room and sat with me on my bed. "Want to tell me about it?"

I shook my head. I wasn't sure how to explain what I'd just dreamed. I knew from the clothes the two people had been wearing that the dream wasn't one of my premonitions, but I had no explanation for who Mathias and Kathryn were or why I would be dreaming about them.

"I think I've been reading too many romance novels." I said, laughing and trying to ease my mother's anxiety. "This one was set in the 1920s I think. Just a boy and a girl. Nothing to worry about."

Mom kissed my forehead. She always worried when my dreams woke me, even when they weren't nightmares or premonitions. "Think you'll go back to sleep tonight?"

"Probably. It wasn't really a bad one." Unless you counted murder as bad, I added silently

"You need to sleep more, baby. Tomorrow's the first day of school and you'll want to be on the ball."

"I'm fine, Mom. Really. It was just weird, not scary and definitely not a premonition."

OK, so that was a lie. Watching that boy drain the life out of his love made my stomach somersault with horror, but I didn't feel like explaining that to my mom in the middle of the night. Despite what he'd done, Mathias didn't strike me as evil or sinister. His obvious grief over what he'd done in my dream hinted at a deeper, purer soul than the act would seem to allow for.

"Okay, okay, I can take a hint. Sleep well, baby. I love you."

"I love you, too, Mom."

I curled onto my side, clutching my pillow after Mom went back to her room where her partner Tawnya was probably waiting for a report of my dream. I knew sleep should have been a dim hope after the dream I'd had, but strangely I didn't feel frightened or threatened by this dream. There was something so compelling about Mathias that I found myself hoping he would be waiting for me when sleep claimed me once again. I closed my eyes, whispering his name and willing him to come to me. When he appeared, waiting at the edge of darkness where dreams live, I reached for him.

***

"Mom, where's my backpack?"

"Where'd you leave it, Mairin?"

That was helpful, I thought. Why was the first day of school always so chaotic? I'd done this at least ten times before and yet I was still running at least fifteen minutes late and I couldn't find my backpack. I dove back into my closet, still on the hunt, hoping it would turn up soon. The last thing I needed was to be late on the first day.

"Mairin, here," Kerry said, bumping the bag against my butt.

"Thanks, sis," I mumbled, digging through the bag to make sure I had everything I needed.

"Can I get a ride?" she asked.

"Sure. Five minutes."

Kerry bolted down the hall to her room. She was excited about starting high school and I didn't have the heart to burst her bubble. Highland Home High School was not the sparkling castle on the hill Kerry thought it would be. It was a cesspool of class warfare and guerrilla tactics that would shame the Taliban.

The two years I'd been at Highland Home had been, to put it mildly, hell. Two years of getting tripped in the hall. Two years of being called a dyke and a lesbo. Two years of pity in the eyes of the teachers who knew about the taunts but who wouldn't risk their jobs by punishing the kids whose families ruled our little town.

The Golden Ones, as I liked to call them, ran Highland Home like a prison camp. The "haves" had it good. The "have-nots" suffered in silence if they knew what was good for them. I tried to be invisible, but when your mother lives with another woman and runs the metaphysical shop downtown, invisible isn't possible.

The best I'd been able to accomplish was transparency. Most of the time the people in Highland Home looked through or past me. There were, of course, some notable exceptions, but I could usually make it through any given day without suffering any permanent damage.

Don't get me wrong, I love Tawnya, my mom's girlfriend, and I wouldn't want Mom to do anything other than what she did at the shop, but I had to admit that my life would be easier if our family were a little more mainstream.

Kerry poked her head into my room. "Ready when you are," she said.

"We're going, Mom," I shouted from the foot of the stairs.

"I'll be at the shop late tonight," she said. "Tawnya will be here when you get home."

Kerry and I slipped into my car and I cringed as the engine roared to life. I knew my mom and Tawnya had saved for ages to help me buy the car, but I also knew it would be just one more thing for the Golden Ones to laugh at. They drove sleek little sports cars. I drove an ancient Chevy Nova that needed a new muffler.

I parked and turned the car off quickly. If I were lucky, no one had noticed the deafening roar of my antique. Sometimes, though, I thought if it weren't for bad luck, I'd have no luck at all. That was surely the case today. Stephanie Bartlet, queen bee of the Golden Ones and her boyfriend, Braden Lambert were already pointing at me and the Nova, laughing uproariously.

"Kerry," I said, "No matter what, remember that high school only lasts four years."

Kerry looked at me like I was losing my mind before she dashed out of the car to join a gaggle of freshman girls clustered around the gym door. I didn't want to be the one to tell my sister the secret of why Stephanie Bartlet had made it her life's goal to make my life miserable. I was actually hoping Kerry would never have to learn first hand what a spiteful and bitter bitch Stephanie was, but I knew better. Someday Kerry would do or say something Stephanie didn't like and Stephanie would delight in spilling family secrets to my sister. I only knew the truth behind the hideous taunts and nasty rumors because Stephanie herself had screamed it at me during a particularly nasty argument we'd had in ninth grade.

I'd always known my parents hadn't had a "normal" marriage. Mom had a girlfriend and Dad had lady friends who sometimes joined the family for trips and holidays. I'd always wondered if Mom married Daddy because of me. She'd gotten pregnant young and although I knew she loved Daddy, I only had to see her with Tawnya to know where here heart truly lay. She'd always called Daddy her best friend and she always made sure to tell me and Kerry that we had been blessings to them both.

For reasons I'd never asked about, around the time Mom got pregnant with me, Daddy had had an affair with Stephanie Bartlet's mother. Stephanie was the result of that affair, though neither the Bartlets nor the Cotes acknowledged the fact. Sometimes I would catch Stephanie staring at me with a bitter and sad expression on her pretty face. I used to think she'd gotten the better half of the deal, growing up with the Bartlet money and name, but I'd seen Stephanie and her family at the summer street fair one year. Stephanie had been standing off to the side, separated from her brothers and parents. She had watched them laugh together with such deep envy that I'd truly pittied her. When Mr. Bartlet finally realized Stephanie wasn't keeping up with the family, he'd shouted at her and both Stephanie and her mother had cringed. I knew Mr. Bartlet was pretty nasty in general, but he seemed to truly enjoy treating Stephanie like a leper. She, in turn, took out her anger on me.

I knew none of the things that happened in the past truly excused Stephanie's behavior toward me, but I did understand her anger. I tried to stay away from her, or at least not give her fuel for her taunts. I hoped Kerry could do the same.

Knowing that delaying the inevitable would only mean more spectators for the insults I could see Stephanie working on, I heaved the Nova's door open and slammed it shut. The ensuing boom couldn't drown out the laughter coming from the crowd gathered around Stephanie and Braden. I kept my head down and headed toward the school.

"And I thought dinosaurs were extinct, Braden," I heard Stephanie shout.

"Apparently they only come out for dykes."

I kept walking. "It isn't worth it," I repeated silently until the door to the school closed behind me, blocking out the Golden Ones' laughter. I knew it wasn't worth getting upset over. I'd learned that lesson the hard way. The more upset I got, the worse the insults got. The more I stood up for myself, the harsher the taunts became.

"She's a worthless bitch, you know," my best friend, Cecelia said, slipping up behind me.

"Yeah, I know. Besides, I like my car. It has character."

"Your car could eat hers for breakfast and crap out a Mini Cooper."

I laughed and hugged Cecelia. "You always know just the right thing to say."

"So how was your last weekend of freedom?" she asked.

"Not bad. Mom and Tawnya took us to the beach. Kerry got burnt, I finished the summer reading list."

"Only you could turn a beach trip into an excuse to do homework."

Cecelia and I stopped at the open door to our homeroom, reluctant to start the school day. She was right. I could turn almost anything into an excuse to do homework. It was the only way I could see for getting out of this town before it sucked me in the way it had my mom. I guess there was nothing wrong with falling in love and having kids, but I was determined to get out of Highland Home and see the world before I let that happen to me. I wanted more out of life and college was the one way I knew I could get it.

"How many applications did you fill out last week?" Cecelia asked. She knew of and approved of my obsession to get out of Highland Home. We planned to go to college together, find our paths to success together and end up married and living next to each other so we could be friends for our entire lives. Sure, it was a hokey dream, but so what?

"A few," I said. Fourteen, I thought.

"Uh huh."

"What about you? How many?"

"Excuse me, ladies," a silky smooth, yet somehow incredibly rough voice broke into our conversation. "Can you tell me where Mr. Stevens' classroom is?"

I looked up and found myself drowning in two pitch black pools of molten heat. My heart stopped. Recognition slammed into me, stealing my breath and my good sense. The vision in designer clothes waiting patiently for me to stop acting like a guppy on land and answer him was the boy from my dream. Fear and desire twisted in my belly and I finally raised my hand to point across the hall.

"Thank you," he said before turning away.

"You're welcome," Cecelia quipped. She waited until my dream had disappeared from view before smacking me in the forehead. "What's wrong with you?"

"Who was that?" I asked, still reeling from literally meeting the man of my dreams.

"How should I know, nitwit? You just blew your chance to ask him, though."

I groaned. "What the heck is wrong with me?"

Cecelia shrugged. "I'm sure he'll be around. Next time, promise me you'll use that enormous brain of yours for something other than a paper weight."

I nodded and followed Cecelia into our homeroom when the bell rang. Cecelia knew about my dreams, but we didn't talk about that stuff often. I knew she was my friend no matter what, but the premonitions made her nervous. I think she worried that one day I would have a dream about her future, or lack of it. What would she say if I told her I'd dreamed of that gorgeous boy last night. Not only did I dream of him, but I dreamed he was a vampire who killed the woman he loved. Cecelia would be supportive, but freaked out. I wasn't willing to do that to her on the first day of school. We were under enough pressure without the metaphysical baggage. We took our usual seats at the back of the room and I tried to sort out what had happened in the hall.

He was gorgeous, sure, but there were other good-looking guys in our school. I let my homeroom teacher drone on while I reconstructed his face in my mind. Deep, dark eyes. Hair like a raven's wing, but with just a touch of curl. Tall, he'd towered over me. I shook my head. What did it matter? He'd find the popular gang soon enough and never think of me again. At least that's what I thought.

***

"We're going to start this year with The Crucible," Mr. Stevens said. The class groaned in unison.

I was settling back, feeling pretty smug because I'd read the play over the summer when the boy from my dreams arrived a few minutes late.

His gaze swept the room as though searching for something, only pausing when he found me at the back of the classroom. The blood rushed to my cheeks and I tried to find anywhere else to look other than those deep black eyes that never left mine as Mr. Stevens explained we were short on books and there would surely be someone willing to share with him. The teacher gestured around the room to the empty seats and I noticed Stephanie Bartlet pat the desk next to her, inviting the new boy to sit with her. I knew if that happened, I was lost. Stephanie would suck this beautiful boy into the Golden Ones and I would never get the chance to know more about him than what the rumor mill would release. To my immense surprise, however, the boy from my dreams ignored Stephanie's invitation and walked surely to the empty seat behind me. He slipped into the desk and I heard Cecelia whisper, "That's going to cost him."

She was right, of course. As queen bee, Stephanie Bartlet was the arbiter of all things cool and popular at Highland Home. If the new guy knew what was good for him, he'd beg her forgiveness and let her accept him into the Golden Ones.

"Class, please welcome Mathias Auer. He'll be joining us this year" Mr. Stevens said.

His name shot a bolt of disbelief through my whole body. It simply wasn't possible for me to have dreamed about the past and have that past walk into my present. My premonitions didn't work that way, or at least they hadn't up to this point. I must have had some odd look on my face because when I looked up, Cecelia was frowning at me.

"What's wrong?" she mouthed.

"Later," I waved her off. I couldn't form coherent thoughts, let alone attempt to share anything with her without getting caught by Mr. Stevens, or worse, Stephanie and her cronies.

What kind of name was Mathias, I wondered idly. I'd never met anyone with that name before and didn't remember even reading it in one of the scores of romance novels I'd read in my life. Mathias...It sounded classy and classical and it certainly fit the reserved and beautiful boy who sat comfortable and silent behind me while the whispers of my classmates erupted around us the moment Mr. Stevens turned his back to continue his lecture.

I jumped when a hand settled on my shoulder. "May I share your book?"

When I turned, Mathias had leaned forward to whisper his request to me and I found myself staring into his dark eyes with little distance between us. I pulled in a deep breath to attempt to calm my thundering heart and caught a whiff of something dark, earthy and tantalizing. The scent caressed my senses, bringing up visions of deep forests and dark nights and it took a moment for me to realize Mathias was still waiting for me to answer him.

"Um, sure," I said. I put my book on his desk.

Mathias lowered his head and began to read along with Mr. Stevens. I stared at the tumble of his loose black curls and was struck by an almost insane desire to run my fingers through his hair. I wondered if his hair was soft or coarse. If it would feel like silk against my fingers. If he would kiss me.

Jeez, where did that thought come from? I blinked and forced myself to return to the present only to realize Mr. Stevens had been trying to get my attention.

"Mairin, would you please pick up with Abigail's lines?" Mr. Stevens said. Stephanie snickered and wound her index finger in a tight circle next to her temple. Great, I thought. One more reason for Stephanie to think I was losing my marbles.

"Yes, Mr. Stevens," I said and then realized I had no idea where we were in the play.

"Here."

I followed the long finger Mathias laid on the page and began to read. I kept my head down, but kept sneaking glances at the boy beside me. He watched me silently, barely glancing at the page to read John Proctor's lines as the characters fought over whether or not John loved Abigail. His voice jolted me each time he spoke, sending little electric thrills down my spine. Mr. Stevens finally started in on his lecture again and I was able to lean away from Mathias. The distance gave me some clarity and let me breathe. What was it with this guy?

I wasn't normally a boy-crazed teenaged girl. Between my desire to go to a good college to escape Highland Home and my efforts to be invisible in order to avoid the Golden Ones, I had rendered myself almost entirely unseen by most of the male population of Highland Home. When you factored in my refusal to act like a stupid twit in order to stroke the egos of the boys who did see me, it left very little interaction with the opposite sex.

There was something about the way Mathias had looked at me in the hall and as he'd walked down the aisle to his seat that made me feel as though he saw more than others. It was as though he could see past the walls I'd built and into the transparent parts of me to find the deepest and most secret places in my soul that I didn't share with anyone. Being seen like that, after years of transparency, left me breathless. I wanted to be near him, to hear his voice, to be lost in the deep chasm of his eyes.

When the bell rang, Mathias rose and stalked from the room, moving with a cat-like grace. He was gone before I was out of my seat.

"Well that was weird," Cecelia said as we headed down the hall to the cafeteria. "What's up with you and the new guy?"

"I wish I knew, Cece," I said. I knew I needed Cecelia's clarity and ability to keep me grounded so I decided to share my dream with her. "I know you don't like the metaphysical stuff, but I've got to tell someone or I'm going to explode."

Cecelia eyed me. "Maire, what's going on?"

"I dreamed of him. Mathias I mean. I dreamed about him last night."

"Well your dreams are premonitions sometimes, right?"

"Yeah, but the dream last night took place in the past, not the future. Mathias..." I stopped. Did I dare tell Cecelia the outcome of the dream? I had to, I decided. Someone else had to know what I was dealing with, no matter how selfish it was of me to dump this stuff on her.

"Mathias what, Maire?"

"He was a vampire in my dream. And he killed a woman I think was his wife."

Cecelia shook her head and laughed. "You're kidding, right? You took that seriously? Come on, Maire, you know you've been reading too many novels when you start dreaming about vampires."

I relaxed and laughed with her. Trust Cecelia to be the one to smack me with a reality check. She was always great for keeping me firmly planted in reality, something I really needed in order to balance out the metaphysical mess that was my daily life.

"You're right, Cece. I gotta stop reading that junk before bed."

Cecelia's reality check might not explain why Mathias had starred in my dream, but it did make me feel better about the vampire part. I mean who didn't think of vampires as dark, mysterious and sexy. Maybe the dream had been somewhat of a premonition that this new boy was coming to our school and my over-charged imagination had superimposed the vampire stuff to amuse my subconscious. I began to feel a bit more normal about the dream and Mathias' appearance as I followed my classmates through the rest of the morning.

Mathias wasn't in any of my other morning classes. I waited impatiently for him to appear, even giving him fifteen minutes of leeway before admitting defeat. The rumor mill was in full production by the time Cecelia and I headed to the cafeteria for lunch. I heard his name whispered by nearly every group I passed and I caught myself watching for him as we traveled with our classmates through the halls.

Cecelia and I left our books with Thomas, Nate and Janet and joined the throng lined up at the lunch counters.

"Did you meet the new guy yet?" I heard a girl in front of us ask her friend.

"No, but he's in my English class. Mr. Stevens said his name was something that starts with an M, but I wasn't really paying attention."

"Mathias," I said without thinking. Cecelia kicked my ankle. As the girl turned toward us, I realized why.

"Oh hell," I thought. It was Stephanie.

"Did you say something to me?" she asked.

"His name is Mathias."

Stephanie looked at me as though I'd grown horns. "And what makes you think I care?"

That was a very good question. I knew every word I said from here on was one more shovelful of dirt from my social grave. Stephanie would not take well to being embarrassed by me about something like the new guy who had snubbed her in English in order to sit near me. The problem was, I couldn't stop myself. It mattered to me that she knew Mathias' name, though I had no idea why. I was about to snap off another ill-conceived retort when I caught sight of someone tall and dark standing beside me.

"I care," his smooth voice was a caress that made me shiver. "It is, after all, my name."

I looked up to find Mathias leaning in close to me. He flashed a cold, brittle smile to Stephanie before turning his back on her. What had been an icy rebuff for Stephanie turned to a warm, inviting smile when Mathias looked at me.

"Would you care to join me for lunch, Mairin?" he asked.

"You know you don't have to eat with the losers, Mathias," Stephanie said, desperation making her voice high and whispery. "You'd be welcome to join us at our table."

Mathias ignored Stephanie and waited for my answer without turning his attention away from me.. Behind his shoulder I could see Stephanie positively seething. She wasn't used to being ignored.

Cecelia pushed me from behind, breaking the spell of disbelief is was under. I coughed in an attempt to cover my apparent break with sanity and reality. "Sure," I said. "Why don't you come sit with us?"

I pointed to the table where Janet sat open-mouthed. Thomas and Nate waved, welcoming smiles plastered on their faces. It wasn't often that one of the beautiful people went out of their way to interact with me or my friends. Mathias nodded once, smiled and headed across the cafeteria.

"Well," Cecelia said, "you must have made some impression in English class."

"Shove it, Cece," I said. I watched as Mathias sat next to Nate, immediately engaging in what looked like a spirited conversation with my friends. I wanted to be happy that this dark stranger had chosen me and my friends, but deep down, I knew the kind of trouble his attention was going to cause for us. When Mathias tired of me and my friends, he would be welcomed into the Golden Ones with open arms. His good looks and obvious wealth made that a no-brainer. The thought of Mathias backing Stephanie's campaign to make me miserable made my chest tight with anguish. Would the taunts and insults be any less painful if they were spoken in his rough, silky voice?

Cecelia pushed me through the line, pulling me back to reality each time I turned to stare at the boy who continued to talk to my friends, but kept watching me. I couldn't take my eyes off him. I wanted to know why he seemed to like me when we'd done nothing more than share a book.

"If you keep gawking, he's going to think you're brain damaged," Cecelia hissed as we walked to the table.

"I can't help it," I said. "How can you look away?"

"He's cute," Cecelia said. "I'll give you that. But he's not really my type."

I shook my head and tried to pull my gaze from the dark eyes that watched each step I took. His smile was wide, welcoming and dazzling. I felt the world around us dim until only he and I existed.

It was a heady feeling to be the center of attention from this amazing and mysterious boy, but there was something sinister underlying every good feeling I'd had about him. In the back of my mind I kept seeing his eyes, dark and cold, above the pale flesh of Kathryn's arm. I heard the wet passage of blood from her body to his lips. I saw her glassy stare when he'd finished with her. No matter what Cecelia had said about too many romance novels, my dream still haunted me and left me to wonder if someday I might not willingly watch this beautiful stranger drain my life away.

I sat down next to Janet, who looked like she was going to burst at the seams if she didn't get to ask me about Mathias soon. The thing was, I didn't know what I could say. "Yeah, we shared a book in English today. Oh and I dreamed about him last night," was all I could think of. As to why he was sitting next to me, smiling at me, trying to engage me in conversation, I had absolutely no idea. All I did know was that each time I heard his voice, my heart stuttered and my breath caught in my throat.

"Mathias was just telling us about Los Angeles," Thomas said. "I can't imagine why anyone would move from someplace exciting like Los Angeles to someplace as dull as here."

"I don't know," Mathias said, looking at me, "I don't think here is dull at all."

***

The rest of the day passed in a blur. Mathias appeared in each of my afternoon classes, sat himself near me and so far as I could tell, spoke to no one but me and my friends. By the end of the day, Stephanie and her cronies were livid and glared daggers at me. Mathias had, not so subtly, rebuffed her and several others four times during various classes and I could see the rumor mill would be full of hateful things about us the next day.

Oddly enough for the first time since middle school, I didn't care what the Golden Ones might say. I was engrossed in the mystery that was Mathias Auer.

"Tell me about Highland Home," he said as we walked from one class to the next.

"There's really not much to tell," I said. "The best part of this crappy town is the beach."

Mathias smiled. "I will agree with you that the beach here is quite pleasant. It was part of the reason I chose to move here."

"Just part?"

The bell rang and we were forced to cut our conversation short. I wondered what else had prompted Mathias, who obviously had wealth and refinement, to choose a provincial New England town like Highland Home over Los Angeles. I wondered, too, where his parents were. He spoke of making choices as though he had no one to whom he answered.

When the final bell rang, Mathias was gone before I could question him further about what had brought him to Highland Home. His parting words had pushed all other questions out of my head.

"I will see you in the morning, Mairin," Mathias said after the bell had rung.

Before I could stop myself, I blurted out, "Why?"

Mathias smiled at me and my heart skipped erratically in my chest. "Because I am not strong enough to deny myself your company," he said and then he was gone.

As I watched him walk down the hall, I realized it didn't matter that I had no idea why this beautiful and mysterious boy was so interested in me. The fact that he was made me feel whole in a way I'd never felt before. He saw me, sought me out, made me feel visible when before I'd always been something of a ghost. It was almost as though Mathias was the sun and through his light the shadows were chased away and I was left revealed. I shook myself out of my reverie and headed for my locker.

"Oooooh, the new boy likes Mairin," Stephanie said, envy dripping from her tongue. "We'll have to start calling them M&M."

The crowd of girls who always surrounded Stephanie laughed loudly before beginning to chant, "M&M. M&M."

I ducked my head and grabbed what I needed from my locker. Cecelia joined me and we headed for my car.

"Tell me everything," she said.

"I don't know what to tell you, Cecelia. You saw him almost as much as I did today."

"Yeah, but he didn't spend the day looking for reasons to get close to me."

A shiver ran down my spine. "He wasn't looking for reasons to get close to me," I said. "I'm sure he was just sticking close to the familiar. Tomorrow he'll realize what a social nonentity I am at this school and jump ship for Stephanie's crowd."

"I doubt that," Cecelia said, but she dropped the interrogation as we headed out to the parking lot.

Between Mathias' parting comment and Cecelia's insistence that Mathias was looking for reasons to be near me, I was completely confused. I would have to concede that Cecelia was right. Mathias had spent the entire day seeking ways to remain by my side. I still had no idea why, but I couldn't deny the truth of that observation.

Mathias' parting words were problematic. What did it mean that he didn't have the strength to stay away from me? There was a weight to those words which made me more than a little uncomfortable. It was almost as though he knew of my dream, of my premonitions and while he felt he had a choice to stay or go, going was the harder of the two options. So hard that he'd rather stay and be in pain than go.

It was a silly fantasy, of course. No one was fated to live any one way or do anything. We all chose our own paths.

When we reached the parking lot, Kerry waited at my car. She looked at me a little strangely but didn't say anything. She climbed into the back seat, leaving the front for Cecelia.

"How was your first day, sis?" I asked.

"OK"

I glanced in the rear view mirror. "Just OK?" I asked.

"Yeah."

I was thinking of pressing Kerry for details when I rounded the corner of the building and damn near ran over Thomas as he charged across parking lot to where a knot of people surrounded one sleek, black car. I didn't really have to look to know it would be Mathias leaning casually against the driver's door. Of course he would drive that little sports car. His clothes probably cost more than my car, why wouldn't his car be worth more than my mom's house? He looked up as I pulled past him and I felt his gaze lock on mine.

"That would be his car," I mumbled.

"What?"

"Mathias' car. He drives that little sports car of course."

"Is that the guy everyone's been talking about today?" Kerry asked.

"I guess so. I wasn't listening," I said.

Kerry was looking over her shoulder. "I think he wants you to stop, Mairin," she said.

I just shook my head and kept going. Beautiful, I could handle. Rich I could handle. I'd grown up in Highland Home, I saw rich and beautiful everyday. Mysterious and new, I could handle. What I couldn't handle was this inexplicable desire Mathias seemed to have for me. It wasn't normal, and I'd had enough of strange for one day. I needed to get away from Mathias and his intensity.

I drove to Cecelia's house in silence. I kept seeing Mathias leaning against his car, a tiny smile pulling the corner of his mouth up. He had been so still amid the chaos of swarming boys and girls who wanted to see his car, to see him. He'd just stood and let them pool around him like moths to a flame. Hadn't I thought of him as a sun, a light to draw everything around him into sharper focus? Why wouldn't he be flames as well? Would he consume me if I let myself get too close? Something about the way he moved, about the way he looked at me, made me think he probably would burn me up. And I'd smile as the flames devoured me.

"Call me later?" Cecelia called as she left the car.

"Yeah." I could tell my brooding silence had bothered her, but Cecelia was never one to push when I wasn't opening up. It was part of why we'd been friends for so long.

She shook her head before turning to her house. I backed out, glancing at Kerry again as I did.

"Wanna tell me what's wrong?" I asked.

She climbed over the seat and then looked at me for a while before she said anything. I let her take her time. Kerry and I were very different people. Where I'd always been kind of solitary and brooding, my sister was open and gregarious. She watched me and dealt with my metaphysical crap as though there were no other way to be. I tried to look out for her, but often that meant keeping a distance so those who sought to hurt me wouldn't notice her. She watched me now as though seeing me for the first time.

"Why didn't you tell me things were so bad for you at school?" she asked finally.

I sighed. I'd hoped it would take a little longer before Kerry had to face the ugly things people said about us, but I'd known, deep down, today would probably be the last day of her childhood.

"I'm surviving," I said. "How about you?"

She shook her head. "Nobody was mean to me, but I heard some girls saying some awful stuff about you."

"Let them, okay Kerr? Don't get into it with them. It isn't worth it. They'll just start in on you too."

"It's not fair," she said.

"Nope."

"No wonder you study so hard. You cant wait to get out of Highland Home."

I reached for her hand. "You're right, Kerr. I'm ready to move on, but I'll never leave you behind. We're sisters. That's forever."

She smiled, but I could see the pain in her eyes. I knew if she tried to stop Stephanie, the Golden Ones would devour her.

"I hate those girls," she said softly.

"Don't hate them, Kerr. Pity them. They don't like themselves very much. That's why they're nasty to me. Just promise to stay out of Stephanie's way, okay?"

Kerry nodded and I hoped she would take my advice. Stephanie Bartlet would destroy my little sister if Kerry pushed her too hard. I couldn't let that happen. Kerry had a chance to have a relatively happy and normal high school career, if I could keep her from getting caught up in the irrational hatred Stephanie had toward me. At least that's what I thought.

Chapter 2

"Mairin, come to me," Mathias whispered.

Mathias stood on the edge of a black abyss. Around him, darkness pressed in, leaving only his luminescent skin glowing in the dark. Between us the way across the abyss lay in ruins. The bridge was gone, the remains crumbled on the edge of the darkness.

"How?" I called, startled by the echo.

"You must have faith, my love. Take the leap. I beg you." Mathias reached for me. "I need you to have faith in me."

"I'm afraid," I said, taking one step toward the yawning crevasse. "What if I fall?"

"I will always catch you, Mairin. Come to me."

My foot hovered over the edge. I was ready to take the leap of faith. Hadn't he proven his worth? Didn't he deserve my faith in him?

"I'm coming Mathias."

Suddenly the sun shot above the horizon behind Mathias, bathing me in its golden light. For a moment I was dazzled by the light and believed it had come from Mathias. It wasn't until Mathias screamed and smoke poured from his chest that I realized the horror of the sun's affect on him. The acrid flames burst forth and consumed him, leaving nothing but ash. The scream built in my throat but the flames leaped across the crevasse and consumed me.

***

My heart thundered in my chest and I lay gasping for breath. I could still feel the flames baking my skin, but the light was gone. The darkness pressed against me like a living thing. I tried to scream, but there wasn't enough air left in my lungs to form the sound. I could still smell the flames, feel their heat buried in the consuming darkness.

"Mairin."

It was his voice. Of course it was. He whispered my name and I held my breath, waiting to hear it again, to hear anything. Nothing came.

My heart began to slow and I realized the distant glow at the edge of my sight was from the alarm clock beside my bed. I could hear the quiet night sounds of our house, and I could hear the soft snoring coming from Mom and Tawnya's room.

I sat up slowly, uncurling my fists and releasing the sheets. At least this time I hadn't screamed. In the weeks since Mathias had come to Highland Home, I had dreamed of him every night. It wasn't that surprising, really, since he still spent his days by my side. The dreams, however, were getting more and more horrifying. This one had been the worst. It was almost as though the dreams in which Mathias killed and consumed the nameless hordes who populated my dreams were more acceptable to me than a dream in which Mathias himself was the victim, even if he took me with him into the inferno. I couldn't grasp the idea of someone or something destroying the amazing soul who was Mathias Auer.

I was definitely losing it. I had no way of separating the Mathias of my dreams from the Mathias who sat behind me in the classes we shared. So what if he was beautiful in a way that simply didn't compare to anyone else. So what if he was soft spoken and articulate. So what if he seemed inordinately interested in me. None of that was sufficient reason for me to be jerking awake in the middle of the night with his voice in my ears.

As much as I wanted there to be a rational explanation for my dreams and for my reaction to Mathias, I had to admit a metaphysical explanation was becoming more reasonable every day. I'd never used words like "fate" or "soul-mate" before, but they were there, on the edge of my thoughts when I was with Mathias. Normal wasn't a word often used to describe me or my family, so why should I think my reaction to and feelings for Mathias would be normal?

My dreams, which had been a terrifying part of most of my life, were now contradictory. In one moment the boy I dreamed of was as wonderfully beautiful in heart and soul as the boy who waited for me outside my homeroom each morning. In the next moment, Mathias was an evil, life-destroying blood sucking monster. Each I night I was forced to watch Mathias wrench men and women out of the darkness and consume them. It wasn't until I stood and watched the monster weep over the bodies of his victims that the horror would recede and I would be left weeping with him. In these dreams, Mathias didn't see me. He didn't speak to me. I was only an observer. I was beginning to wonder what the difference was between the horror-filled dreams and the ones in which Mathias did see me and speak to me. It was almost as though some of my dreams were his memories, though that was impossible, of course.

During the day the boy who haunted my dreams treated me like a precious possession which must be treasured and protected. He had even taken to running interference between me and the Golden Ones, though I'd begged him not to bother. Despite my protests that his interference would only make things worse, Mathias continued to be somewhat over protective. It was annoying actually. I'd always taken care of myself and the fact that he wouldn't just leave the issue lie, drove me right up a wall. The problem was, it was hard for me to stay angry with him once he'd turned his amazing smile on me. When that happened, I'd forget what I was angry about until he did it again.

I heard Mom coming down the hall and squinted against the light I knew would soon flood my room. She always knew when I had bad dreams, even when I didn't scream. I always wondered what woke her on the nights I had nightmares. I thought it might be some unconscious fear that if she didn't ask me what I'd dreamed, she'd learn of a premonition too late to do anything about it. The door to the hall opened and Mom stood silhouetted in the glare.

"Mairin, honey, what was it tonight?" She asked. She always asked what I dreamed, half hopeful and half afraid of what I'd say.

"Nothing, Mom. Just a regular bad dream."

"Are you sure, Maire? You've been having an awful lot of these dreams lately."

"I'm sure. They're just dreams mom. So far not one of them has proven to be a premonition." That much was true. During the day I had never seen Mathias stalking barmaids or shepherds so he could drink their blood. I certainly hadn't seen him burst into flames in the sunlight either.

"Kerry tells me you've been spending a lot of time with a new boy at school. Is he the reason for your dreams?"

I didn't know how to answer that. Mathias was very much the reason my dreams were as vivid and frequent as they had been lately, but I refused to believe what I was dreaming. Mathias was not the evil creature who stalked in my dreams.

"Definitely not," I said. "He's just a nice guy who hasn't yet figured out that hanging with me is social suicide at Highland Home High School."

"I'm sure that's not true, Mairin."

I hugged Mom. I'd never asked her about Daddy and Stephanie's mother so I didn't know if she knew why the Bartlets had such a deep and abiding hatred of our family. The middle of the night certainly wasn't the time to ask her either.

"Do you want Tawnya to clear the energy in your room tomorrow?"

I shook my head. "You said you needed her at the shop tomorrow. That means she has readings to do. No sense in her wearing herself out at home when there are paying clients. I'll burn some sage when I get home from school."

Mom watched me for a moment from the doorway before nodding. I could tell she wasn't happy with my explanation of the dream or my refusal to let Tawnya clear my room, but she couldn't see any way to make me let her get her way without feeling like the wicked witch mom.

"Well, try to get some sleep, OK? It's only three thirty."

"Sure Mom. Right back to sleep."

The door closed behind her and I stared into the sudden darkness. We both knew I wouldn't be sleeping any more that night.

The night terrors had started when I was five. For years, I'd screamed myself awake with no memory of the dream. It got worse later when I could remember the dreams because I realized the dreams were about things that would happen later. The premonitions may not have begun with the dream of my father's car wreck, but that was the first one I remembered. After Daddy's funeral, I stopped sleeping. It took about a week for my mom to realize I wasn't sleeping for more than a few minutes at a time. Not that Mom wasn't paying attention to me, but she was dealing with the death of her best friend and trying to handle two girls on her own in a town where she was a pariah because of her choice of love partners. When she did figure it out, she took me first to a psychologist and then to a psychic. The shrink said I was grieving. The psychic said I was having premonitions. My mom sided with both of them and I went through years of psychoanalysis and equally long years of classes taught by various psychics Mom found through her metaphysical business.

The outcome of all the analysis and learning was that I dreaded sleeping and the Golden Ones had one more thing to scream at me in the halls. Stephanie saw me coming out of my shrink's office once and added "nut job" to her repertoire of insults. Later, when Branden's family hired my mom as a fortune teller at one of their charity parties, "freak" became the Golden Ones' favorite epithet.

I watched the sun rise before I gave up pretending to go back go sleep. The light bleeding slowly into the town before bursting over the horizon forcibly reminded me of my dream. I shuddered and tried to forget the sight of Mathias' beloved face crumbling to dust. I shook myself and got up to get ready for school. I was waiting for Kerry to finish her breakfast when I noticed a pale blue glow around her head and shoulders.

"Quit staring at me, Maire. It's creepy."

"What? Oh, sorry."

"What are you looking at anyway," Kerry asked, brushing off her blouse. "Did I spill something?"

I shook my head. "Nothing. I didn't sleep much last night. My brain must have stopped."

"What did you dream?" Kerry's eyes were wide. I hated seeing that look on my kid sister's face. Ever since she'd found out that I'd dreamed of our dad's accident, she'd hounded me about my dreams almost as much as Mom did.

"Nothing." I laughed at the disbelieving look Kerry shot me. "Really, sis. It wasn't a premonition. I promise." I refused to believe Mathias could be burned to cinders by the sun, so there was no way the dream had been a premonition.

"I still think you should let Tawnya clear your room, honey," Mom said, patting my shoulder as she edged past me to get to the coffee pot.

I shook my head. "Maybe tomorrow, Mom. She needs her strength for your clients."

Mom huffed and started fixing her coffee. I watched her familiar movements fondly before I realized she had that same blue glow that Kerry had.

"Wow, I must be really tired," I said.

"Why?" Mom asked, turning worried eyes my way.

"You and Kerry have blue halos today." I rubbed my eyes, but the blue glows didn't fade.

"Blue halos?"

I nodded. "I'm sure it's just sleep deprivation. I don't have a headache or anything."

Mom stared at me without saying anything. She shook her head before she turned to finish fixing her coffee. She stopped to kiss Tawnya's cheek when the other woman found her way to the kitchen.

"Now that's weird," I said. "Tawnya's halo is gold."

Tawnya's head snapped around. "What halo?"

"I didn't sleep last night. I'm foggy this morning and apparently my brain wants pretty colors. Mom and Kerry are blue and you're gold, Tawnya."

Mom felt my forehead. "You're not warm," she said. "Are you sure you don't want to stay home today?"

"Positive." Staying home would mean a day without Mathias. Much as I hated to admit it, seeing him was the one bright spot on an otherwise dark and dreary social calendar.

"If you change your mind, I don't want you driving home. Call me and I'll come get you."

"I promise, Mom," I poked Kerry. "Come on, sis. Time to get going."

Kerry pounded up the stairs, leaving me with Mom and Tawnya.

"Maire, I'm worried," Mom started. "First all the nightmares and now you're seeing colors around us."

"I'm fine, mom. You know I get a little wonky when I don't sleep."

Tawnya hugged Mom and then me. "Loraine, if something was wrong, Mairin would say so," she looked at me, something hard glinting in her eyes. "Right, Mairin?"

"Right," I said. "The halos are probably nothing. I'm sure they'll be gone by the time I get home."

"OK I know when I'm outnumbered," Mom said, leaning back into Tawnya's arms. "Just be careful driving, OK?"

I hugged her. "Always."

I pulled the Nova into a space and shut the engine down quickly. We were early, so there weren't as many people in the parking lot as there usually were when I arrived at the school. It was painfully easy to find Mathias' car in the open lot.

"That guy is waving at you again, Maire," Kerry said. "You've been spending a lot of time with him, haven't you."

Something in her tone made me look more closely at my sister. "His name is Mathias, Sis," I said. "You don't like him, do you?"

Kerry shook her head. "I don't know what it is about him, but I don't. Sorry, Maire."

I watched Kerry mulling over whatever else she thought she wanted to say. I wanted to hug her, tell her I was fine, that nothing was going on, but I just couldn't. Not when I couldn't be sure the words were true. Mathias hadn't done anything remotely ungentlemanly toward me, but sometimes I caught him watching me with such intensity that I wondered what plans he had but hadn't shared with me.

"Just be careful, OK Maire?" she said. "You might be my big sister, but if I have to, I'll defend your honor."

I laughed. "Well, I don't know how I feel about that," I said. "I kind of think it's supposed to be the other way around."

"I love you, Maire."

"Love you too, Kerr."

I turned to push the Nova's door open, only to find Mathias had beat me to it. He stood back, swept down in a courtly bow. All I could do was stare at the top of his head until Kerry shoved me. Whether she liked Mathias or not, my sister wasn't going to pass up a chance to needle me for being a goofball.

"Good morning, Mairin," he said. He held out his hand and I took it. Touching Mathias was like touching a live electric fence. My nerves jumped and sang in chorus with my thundering heart. It was a strangely pleasant feeling.

"Good morning," I mumbled.

I stood stupidly next to my car, staring at the gloriously beautiful features of this amazing boy. His high cheekbones, dark eyes and dark hair blended into a face I knew would be imprinted on my brain for eternity. The pale gold glow I could now see only made him more painfully gorgeous. I began to feel just a little self conscious standing next to him.

I knew I wasn't a looker. My mousy brown hair and green eyes were pretty enough, but I was nowhere near as stunning as some of the other girls at Highland Home High. Even Cecelia's blond, blue-eyed good looks were something I was used to being eclipsed by. Standing with Mathias made me feel down right hideous sometimes. The only thing which made me feel better about being surrounded by his stunning beauty was how Mathias looked at me. When I saw myself reflected in his black eyes, I was just as stunning as he was. Mathias looked at me as though he'd never before seen a woman. He watched me as if I were his sun.

"May I walk you to class, today?" he asked.

"Um, sure," I said. "Are you sure you want to, though? You could probably still salvage some kind of social status with the Golden Ones if you don't hang out with me."

Mathias' laugh was like someone had made rough, watered silk into a sound. "I think my social standing is in no jeopardy. I rather prefer your company to the-- what did you call them?"

"The Golden Ones."

"Yes, them."

I looked at this glorious boy and my tongue slipped ahead of my brain. Mathias always had that effect on me. "Why?" I blurted before I could stop myself.

Mathias brushed the back of his hand against my cheek. "I thought I explained myself previously Mairin. I like you."

"Who are you?" I asked, resisting the urge to lean into his hand where it still caressed my face.

"I am a planet orbiting my sun," He whispered, forcing me to step closer to hear him. "I am only Mathias."

He took my hand, holding it when the electrical current made me pull back. "Shall we go to your classroom?" he asked. "I promise to answer any questions you ask if you'll allow me to accompany you today."

My curiosity got the better of me and I let him walk me to my homeroom. Cecelia saw us coming and ducked into the classroom so I couldn't use her as an excuse to get away from Mathias. I'd have to have a talk with her about that later. Friends weren't supposed to desert each other just because beautiful boys came into the picture. I suppose she could say the same to me, but Cecelia seemed glad I was spending time with Mathias.

"I don't believe you have no questions for me, Mairin," he said, leaning against the wall. "I can see them whistling around behind those beautiful green eyes of yours."

I felt the blood rush to my face. Great, just great. I knew I looked like a boiled tomato when I blushed. The blood in my cheeks did horrible things to my pale complexion. Mathias watched me carefully before placing his palm against my cheek. His palm felt wonderfully cool against my heated skin and I sighed.

"Ask me one question before you burst," he said.

"What brought you to Highland Home?" I whispered, remembering he'd once said the beach had been only part of his reason for choosing to come to this town.

"Ah, that is an interesting question to begin with," he said, trailing his knuckles across my cheek and jaw. I was suddenly and terrifyingly reminded of the first dream I'd had of Mathias. He'd caressed Kathryn's face just that way. I shuddered and turned my face away. Mathias smiled and dropped his hand to his side. "The short answer is that the company I own moved it's operations near here."

"The short answer?" I said. "What's the long answer?"

The bell rang and Mathias smiled. "The long answer will have to wait." he pushed away from the wall and reached for my hand. I was still reeling from the electrical currents that kept coming each time he touched me when I realized he'd lifted my hand to his lips and kissed the back of it. "Until later, Mairin."

I stood, stunned and unable to move. Mathias' normally reserved manners had slipped significantly today. Never before had he so blatantly sought to touch me. The nerves on the back of my hand still sang with the electricity left by his lips.

I watched him cross the hall to Mr. Stevens' room, but I couldn't seem to move. It wasn't until I heard the high-pitched screaming laugh of Stephanie Bartlet echoing behind me that my paralysis broke.

"So M&M is going to be a thing, I see," she said as I took my seat beside Cecelia.

"Cram it Stephanie," Cecelia said.

"No," I whispered to my best friend. "Let her go or it'll just get worse."

It was too late, of course. Stephanie sauntered down the aisle to stand next to me. "What has happened in the last twenty four hours that you seem to think it's OK to speak to me?" she asked.

"Nothing, Stephanie," I said. "Just drop it, OK?"

"So now you're giving me orders?"

"No, I just don't want to get into this with you."

"Well I do," Cecelia said. "You're a bitch and you're just jealous that Mathias likes Mairin and not you."

"Cecelia, no."

Cecelia stood up as Stephanie leaned over me to get closer to her. "You really might want to be careful of what you say right now, Cecelia," Stephanie said. "We wouldn't want to have to call your dad, the janitor, to clean up your blood when I knock out your teeth."

I flinched. Stephanie always went too far. For that matter, so did Cecelia. I wasn't going to let this go any farther, not over me. Before I could think it through, I shoved Stephanie. Overbalanced as she was from leaning across my desk, she went flying, landing in an undignified heap next to my desk. From somewhere behind me, I heard someone laugh and I ground my teeth. This day was getting better all the time.

"Miss Bartlet, why are you on the floor?" my homeroom teacher asked.

"Mairin shoved me."

"No she didn't," Cecelia said. "Stephanie tripped."

I watched as the teacher weighed the benefits of giving me detention for something she knew Stephanie probably deserved against letting Cecelia's lie suffice. The lie won.

"Please take your seat, Miss Bartlet."

"But, she shoved me."

"I asked you to please take your seat. Do I need to send you to the office for a detention slip, Miss Bartlet?"

Stephanie stomped back to her desk, turning to glare at me. I knew I'd pay for what I'd done, but it had felt so good that I didn't care.

"What was that about?" I whispered to Cecelia while the secretary read the announcements.

"I'm sick of her, that's all. I have never understood why you let her get away with being such a bitch."

"It's not worth the stress of dealing with detention and the hit Mom's shop would take if the Bartlets decided to shut her down."

Cecelia shook her head. "I couldn't do it, Maire. You're a saint."

"No, just practical."

"So what was with the kiss on the hand thing out in the hall?"

"Saw that, did you?"

"Well, yeah. I think half the school saw it."

I didn't know how to answer Cecelia. I was still reeling from the kiss myself. "I wish I knew."

"Think you guys will ever go on a real date?"

"Who knows. He's not like the other guys here. He's polite. He listens to me. And so far the most sexually forward thing he's done is kiss the back of my hand."

"You like him."

I sighed. "Yeah, Cece. I like him."

"Well, it's about time. You've let Stephanie and her cronies keep you from liking anyone, I was convinced you'd graduate from high school without a single date and definitely as a virgin."

"Cece!"

"Well, it's true, Maïre. You haven't been on a date since that one time you and Thomas went to the movies in ninth grade."

I laughed, remembering the strangely formal kiss Thomas had tried to give me at the end of the date. From then on, we'd decided we were definitely better friends than we would be as boyfriend and girlfriend.

"So I don't date. Neither do you."

"Yeah, well, there is that."

"Maybe we should focus on finding you someone to date. Then if Mathias actually asks me out, we can double. Of course since I doubt Mathias is going to ask me out, I think we're safe for a while."

Chapter 3

"You really own a pharmaceutical company?" I asked.

Mathias nodded. "I was very young when my parents died. I lived with a guardian over the years, but decided recently I was quite old enough to live on my own. When the board of directors wanted to move the headquarters to the east coast, I thought a change of scenery would be good for me."

I leaned back in my chair, suddenly aware that I was leaning into Mathias as we talked amid the clamor of the cafeteria. Why was I always leaning in, getting closer to this boy? Part of me thought he purposely spoke in a softer tone so I would have to lean in, but that would mean he wanted me to be closer to him.

Since the morning he'd kissed my hand, Mathias had continued his campaign to get closer to me physically. It was rare now for him to not hold my hand as we walked from one class to another. He often brushed his knuckles along my jaw, a caress which never failed to make me tremble with a combination of desire and terror. The one thing he'd never attempted was to kiss me. I found myself watching his lips as he spoke and fantasizing about how they would feel against my own.

I blinked slowly, realizing I'd drifted away again. Mathias' bemused smile made me wonder how long I'd been gone.

"Sorry," I said sheepishly, "I didn't sleep well last night.

"I apologize," he said. "I hope your dreams this evening are more pleasant."

"I never said anything about dreams," I said defensively.

"I simply assumed that was the cause of your poor rest, Mairin,"

"Oh." I felt the blood rush to my cheeks. "I'm a little touchy about my dreams."

"I see that. Would you care to share the reason you're 'touchy' about your dreams?"

Mathias' tone and posture invited confidence, but I didn't know how to explain my dreams to people without them either running away or feeling sorry for me because they thought I was crazy. I especially didn't feel prepared to discuss my dreams with the most recent star of them.

I shook my head. "Not yet."

Mathias smiled. "I heard what happened between you and Stephanie," he said, changing the subject.

"Oh," I'd hoped the story hadn't made the rounds since I hadn't heard any buzz about it. Even Stephanie seemed determined that the story wouldn't get out. I'd been sure she would find a way to make me the villain and to play the helpless damsel, but she hadn't even retaliated.

"I'm sure whatever you heard was exaggerated."

Mathias took my hand, rubbing his thumb over the back of it before turning it over to trace the lines on my palm. I was getting used to the electrical current that passed between us when Mathias touched me, but I still couldn't fathom why he kept reaching for me.

"What I heard was that you shoved that horrible girl for picking on your friend Cecelia," Mathias said. "You should be proud to stand up for your friends."

I nodded, unable to speak. I put my other hand over his to stop him from tracing his fingers over my palm. There was something far too intimate in that act. It was as though he were memorizing parts of my past and future by tracing the lines put there by the Divine. Instead of drawing away as he often did when I touched him, Mathias let me turn his hand palm up. His hand was large with a square palm and long fingers. My hand was dwarfed beside his. I lightly trailed my fingertips over the hills and valleys of his cupped palm, smiling when Mathias shuddered. It was nice to know my touch had the same effect on him as his did on me. I watched the path my fingers took, lost in the sensation of the rough callouses and smooth hidden places on his palm. I was fascinated by his hand and it took me some time before I realized why Mathias' palm looked so strange.

"That's weird," I said.

"What is?"

"Your palm is almost completely smooth. Hardly any lines."

Mathias slowly pulled his hand from mine, laying it palm down on his knee. I could tell he tried to do it without hurting my feelings, but I was hurt just the same. Mathias had shunned the Golden Ones in favor of me and my friends. He had begun to let his cool reserve and formal distance slip so he could get closer to me, but touch, the most basic human connection, had to be only on his terms. I crossed my arms, tucking my hands away as much to keep Mathias from taking them as to restrain myself from reaching for him again.

"You really should let Mairin read your palm, Mathias," Stephanie said, leaning over my shoulder to take his hand and pull it closer to me.

"Don't touch me, please," Mathias said. I heard the low timbre of a growl in his voice and it set my teeth on edge. It was a sound I had heard in my dreams, one that often meant death was coming. In the present, Mathias jerked his hand out of Stephanie's grasp and rubbed it against his leg as though he'd touched something nasty.

"But the little freak is so good at fortune telling, aren't you?" Stephanie's tone was drenched in hate and anger. "Didn't you predict your daddy's death? Too bad you didn't tell anyone until after it happened."

I heard Cecelia gasp and the din of conversation in the cafeteria dimmed until I couldn't hear anything but my heart beating frantically in my chest. So this was the price for embarrassing Stephanie in our homeroom. Only Stephanie in her quest for ways to break me would bring up our father in such a hateful manner. I could see that even her cronies, who likely didn't understand the depth of Stephanie's barb, were shocked and beginning to slink away so they wouldn't get caught in the crossfire. I tried to slow my heart and regain some measure of control before my tongue got ahead of my brain. I had a nasty retort poised on the tip of my tongue, but Mathias beat me to it.

As the last syllable passed Stephanie's lips, Mathias stood and stepped between me and the grinning Golden One. The growl I'd heard a hint of a moment earlier was in full blossom on his beautiful lips. My awareness focused narrowly until I could feel the oppressive darkness of my dreams closing in. His voice, deepened and destroyed by the growl, called to me out of the darkness. The animal nature of the sound left goosebumps raised on my arms and neck and set my heart tripping ever faster in my chest. I leaned around his body so I could see Stephanie and I lay my hand against his back. My heart thundered as the possibility of my dreams being premonitions became a very real thing. I hoped to calm Mathias before the beast in his voice burst forth and devoured my arch nemesis, taking my heart and future happiness with her.

"Apologize," he demanded before I could tell him I was okay and that starting a fight with Stephanie wasn't worth the trouble it would bring later.

Stephanie stumbled back, obviously terrified by the ferocity of Mathias' tone. "I'm...I'm sorry," she said. Her face was blanched white except for two spots of red high on her cheeks. From my subconscious a stream of similar faces burst forth. Every victim I'd dreamed of had looked as Stephanie did now.

"Now go," Mathias said softly. Stephanie turned and ran.

I watched the normally icily composed girl flee and felt a stab of pity for her. First I'd shoved her and now Mathias had terrified her. Even Stephanie didn't deserve that kind of harsh treatment. Mathias was seated across from me, shredding his napkin before I found my voice.

"What the hell was that?" I demanded.

"She insulted you."

"And you decided to scare the living crap out of her in return?"

"I didn't intend to frighten her, only to elicit the apology you deserved." His reasonable tone irritated me. This was the cold, distant Mathias of my nightmares. The monster who could kill, feed and leave the corpse on the cobblestones.

He might be calm and cool but I was furious. I wasn't some shrinking violet who needed a knight in shining armor to defend her against a wicked witch. I was perfectly capable of fighting my own battles or choosing which battles weren't worth the fight. I'd done it for the first sixteen years of my life. Just because this boy had appeared in my life didn't mean I was suddenly incapable of taking care of business.

I stood up. "Well, I don't appreciate what you did." I was shaking with what I thought was anger, though if I was truly honest with myself was probably closer to adrenalin. I had to acknowledge that there was a very real possibility that I was screaming at a dangerous monster and that my dreams really were Mathias' memories. Despite that realization, I didn't care. If Mathias thought he could sweep into my life and turn it upside down without a response from me, he was sadly mistaken.

I realized everyone in the cafeteria had stopped their own conversations to witness my meltdown, but I didn't care that I was the center of attention. If I was going to spend time with Mathias, he was going to have to learn that I didn't need him to fight my battles for me. I turned to stalk out of the cafeteria, but Mathias' hand on my arm stopped me.

"I am sorry, Mairin," Mathias said. "I will not interfere again."

He looked so contrite that my anger dissolved in a single, sudden moment. How could I stay mad when I preferred his smile to the sad look he was giving me now? "Well, yeah then," I said. "That's probably a good idea."

The bell rang, saving me from further embarrassing myself. I both loved and hated the effect Mathias had on me. His ability to take me from fury to love with only one look was disconcerting.

"Shall we go to class?" Mathias asked.

I nodded and let him lead me out of the cafeteria. It dawned on me as we walked that the golden halo around Mathias had darkened during his confrontation with Stephanie and was still darker now than it had been that morning. I filed that away as something to talk to my mom about later. In fact I needed to talk about the halos in general. The variety of colors, or lack thereof, was getting weird, especially when I compared the colors I saw to the people they were attached to. Stephanie's boyfriend, Braden, had a muddy green halo. It was the only one of that color I'd seen. Most people's halos were some shade of blue. And then there was the gold halo I saw around Tawnya and Mathias. I was sure the colors had some meaning, but I couldn't imagine what it might be.

"So what other questions do you want me to answer about myself," Mathias asked. "Or is it my turn?"

"Ask away," I said, collecting my thoughts and focusing on Mathias. "I'm sure my life isn't nearly as interesting as yours."

"I think you underestimate the level of interest I have in you...your life."

I felt the blood rush to my cheeks again. "You talk to me like I'm the most interesting person you've ever met. I know that can't be true."

"I won't argue that particular point with you, Mairin. Suffice it to say that right now there is nothing in this world so interesting to me as you."

"Why do you say things like that?"

"Because they're true. I will always endeavor to tell you the truth Mairin."

"I guess we'll have to agree to disagree on the concept of how interesting I am."

"Certainly," he said, taking my hand again and holding it to his lips. The electricity flowed and I wondered if my face could possibly get any redder.

"Don't do that," I whispered.

"Do what?"

"When you do that...kiss my hand...I feel like a princess in a fairy tale. Boys don't do things like that anymore."

Mathias smiled broadly. "I am not like the other boys."

"You can say that again," I clapped a hand over my mouth. "Dammit, you did it again."

"What have I done now?" Mathias' lips twitched. I knew he was laughing at me.

"I have no filter around you. I just say whatever comes to mind. It's extremely annoying."

"I find it both refreshing and charming."

"You would. You're not the one spilling state secrets."

Mathias frowned. "I would prefer we had no secrets."

Something about the way he said it, made me think he referred to his own secrets rather than mine. Certainly, I'd been unable to hide anything from him.

"You said you wanted to ask me questions. Ask away."

He smiled at my not so subtle change of subject. "I truly have only one question right now."

"What?"

"Will you go to the pep rally and football game with me this evening?"

I stopped in the hall, causing a pile up of epic proportions as the students streaming down the hall stopped with me. Several people cursed and pushed past us. The question was so mundane, so normal, after the scene in the cafeteria and the electricity of his touch that I couldn't focus on anything but the one question I'd resisted asking since Mathias had appeared in my life.

"Why do you want to be with me?" I asked.

"I don't know," Mathias said so softly I wasn't certain I'd actually heard those words. "I want to know you," he said more loudly, casting further doubt on his first statement. He pulled me to the side of the hall to allow the pile up to move past us.

I shook my head. "I don't get it."

"What don't you get?" Mathias leaned against the wall, pinning me under his body while not actually touching me. My heart skipped a beat or two.

"I'm nothing special," I touched his lips to halt his protest. "You're the most amazing, different and interesting person I've ever met. You're smart, articulate, beautiful and perfect. What makes you want to know me?"

Mathias laughed. "I must say, you do have a highly exaggerated idea of who I am, Mairin. But to answer your question, that you do not think you are interesting is why I think you are. You are open and honest in a way that speaks to my very soul. There is something supremely comforting about your presence and despite the fact that my horrifyingly selfish desire to be with you is likely not in your best interest, I find I am unable to deny myself your company." He stared at me until I shivered. "Will you grant me the honor of allowing me to escort you to the pep rally and football game this evening?"

"Determined, aren't you?"

"You have no idea," he said. The smile that pulled the corners of his mouth up made me gasp. Each time I thought he could be no more fascinating, he showed me one more thing, one more reason I wanted to be near him. I realized I'd give almost anything to see that smile every day of my life.

"You'll have to meet my mom and Tawnya first," I said, knowing I'd probably doomed myself to another Friday night at home alone. "Are you sure you're up to that?"

"I think I can handle your mother and her partner," he said. Something in the way he said partner made me think he already knew Mom and Tawnya were more than business partners.

"Then if Mom says it's okay, I'll go with you. Even if I don't get it."

Mathias' smile broadened a bit and he leaned forward as though he were going to kiss me. My heart stopped and my eyes closed as I waited to discover if his lips tasted as sweet as I imagined they would.

"Mr. Auer, Miss Cote, don't you have a class to go to?" the assistant principal asked.

The moment slipped away and I cursed. Disappointment flooded my body, leaving me weak and aggravated. Mathias pulled me toward our class, smiling broadly and refusing to release my hand. The smug bastard acted as though he knew exactly what he'd done to my state of mind and was proud of himself. I didn't hear a word from our teacher for the next hour. I was too lost in a daydream of kissing Mathias until we were both breathless and flushed.

When the final bell rang, Cecelia, Kerry and I made a beeline for my car. I didn't stop to look for Mathias, nor had I told Cecelia about the invitation to the pep rally and game. I wasn't ready for the inquisition from Cecelia and I didn't want to risk running into Stephanie and her friends before I could escape school grounds. The more I thought about the confrontation in the cafeteria, the more uncomfortable it made me. In the cafeteria Mathias had, for the first time since his arrival in my daytime world, behaved in a way which undeniably tied him to the monster of my nights. That growl, the offensive stance, and the terror he'd instilled in Stephanie had made it clear there was so much more to this boy than the cool, reserved facade he hid behind. I was afraid, not so much of Mathias, but of myself. Night after night I watched Mathias devour lives and yet each day I hoped to see him. What did it say about me that I was seemingly willing to overlook the death of others so I could love this beautiful boy?

"Mairin."

His voice stopped me dead. A shiver ran down my spine and the hair on my neck stood on end. How did he do that?

Kerry and Cecelia flanked me like soldiers about to do battle or bodyguards. What was it about Mathias that either drew people to him or repelled them with such force? And why did I feel like I was on the wrong side of that equation?

"Mathias, I'd like you to meet my sister. Kerry, this is Mathias."

Kerry backed away from Mathias' outstretched hand. "Hi," she said softly. I'd never seen Kerry react to anyone like that. Usually my sister was the more gregarious of the two of us.

"A pleasure to meet you, Kerry." Mathias turned to me. "Have you forgotten that I agreed to meet your family before the game tonight?"

"No," I said. "But you seem to know everything about me. I figured you knew where my mom's shop was."

His smile told me he knew that wasn't why I hadn't waited for him. If I didn't know that nearly every thought I ever had passed over my face, I'd think Mathias was a mind reader. The truth was, he saw me in ways no one else tried to. He was perceptive to a fault and I sucked at hiding anything I thought or felt.

"I do not, actually," he said. "Shall I follow you?"

***

"Why didn't you tell me Mathias asked you to the game tonight?" Cecelia demanded.

"It just happened, Cece. I didn't expect him to pounce on me in the parking lot."

Cecelia huffed. I could tell she thought I was keeping secrets, but the truth was, I didn't know what to do about Mathias. No matter how wonderful he was in person, everything he did was superimposed over the horror he was in my nightmares. Every time I screamed myself awake after the Mathias in my dreams had destroyed another life, I swore I would ignore him at school the next day. Then I would see him in person and I would be unable to remember the monster. I could only see the thoughtful and sensitive boy who was determined to be a part of my life.

"I don't think you should go out with him, Maire," Kerry said.

"Why not?"

"I just don't like him. There's something weird about him and I think he's...well I don't think he's good for you."

"I'll take it under advisement," I said, trying to make a joke of her concerns, but I couldn't ignore the fact that I'd had the same thought.

"Don't be too hard on your sister, Kerry," Cecelia said. "She hasn't had a date in a while."

"Bitch," I snapped, laughing.

The moment to consider Kerry's thoughts passed, but I could see when I glanced in the rear view mirror that she hadn't given up her warning.

"Can you drop me at the house, Mairin," Kerry said. "I've got homework."

Chapter 4

The scent of sage, lavender, and peppermint flowed out of my mom's shop in a cloud that always hovered on the edge of overpowering. New age music played softly in the background and the bell above the door chimed, alerting the occupants that visitors from the physical realm had arrived.

The Astral Plane was a charming mixture of old fashioned furniture and new age religion. Mom had opened the shop after Daddy's accident. It gave her something to do and was a way to keep food on the table and pay the mortgage. No matter how much crap I took about the shop from Stephanie and her cronies, I wouldn't want Mom to do anything else. Running The Astral Plane was what my mom loved doing. I sometimes thought she saw the shop as a way of staying connected to Daddy since his insurance money had paid for it. I wouldn't take that from her for anything.

Mom dashed through the curtain from the stockroom when she heard the bell, stopping short when she saw Mathias standing next to me. I guess I couldn't blame her. It wasn't everyday I brought a beautiful stranger over to meet her.

"Hi baby," she said, hugging me quickly. "Where's your sister?"

"I dropped her at the house. She said she wanted to get started on her homework so she could go to the pep rally tonight."

"And who's your friend?" she asked, eying Mathias.

"Mathias, this is my mom, Loraine. Mom, this is Mathias Auer. He's new to Highland Home."

Mathias bowed slightly, but didn't offer his hand to my mom. "It is a pleasure to meet you, Ms. Cote," he said, clasping his hands behind his back. "Your daughter speaks very highly of you."

"Such pretty manners," Mom said. "I'm glad to meet you, too."

I shook my head. This was getting a little too weird. Sure, Mom wasn't used to me bringing boys to meet her, but she was acting really strange. For that matter, so was Mathias. What was with the formality? I half expected Mathias to ask my mother's permission to court me.

"Mathias asked me to go to the pep rally and football game tonight. Can I go?"

"Who's here, Loraine?" Tawnya called from the reading room in the back of the shop.

"It's Mairin and her friend. Come on out and meet him."

Tawnya turned the corner and stopped short. Her eyes grew wide and something about the way she looked at Mathias made me think I was about to have a fight on my hands when I came to spending time with him.

She walked forward, her hand outstretched. "I'm Tawnya, Loraine's partner."

Mathias smiled and bowed. "Mathias Auer. I'm pleased to meet all of Mairin's family."

Mom and I watched Tawnya and Mathias stare each other down. I had no idea what was going on, but I could tell Mathias was getting upset. His halo, which had been light gold, rather pale when compared to the vibrant, pulsing gold of Tawnya's, was darkening. I put my hand on his arm, hoping to head off any reaction which might make Mom decided I couldn't go out with Mathias.

"So can I go, Mom?" I prompted

"What?" Mom shook herself. "Go where?" I realized that Mom had been dazzled by the exchange between Mathias and Tawnya. I was struck, as I often was, by the fact that of all the people in the family who should have had psychic abilities, my mother was the least sensitive of any of us. That she was locked up by Mathias' presence and Tawnya's reaction to him made me wonder what I was missing because my own abilities tended to filter out other psychics and their affects.

"To the school tonight. With Mathias?" I prompted.

"No," Tawnya said.

I looked at her. Tawnya had never behaved like this before. She'd always left the raising of me and my sister strictly to my mom, even though she'd been in our lives from the very beginning.

"Why not?" I demanded.

"Mairin, I don't wish to cause discord in your family...."

"You shut up," I snapped at Mathias. I wasn't going to let him butt into this battle the way he had with Stephanie. Manners be damned, Tawnya was going to give me an answer.

"Mairin!" Mom was looking at me as though I'd lost my mind. I couldn't tell if she was more upset with me for questioning Tawnya or snapping at Mathias. Of course it didn't really matter which it was. There was no going back.

"I want to know why," I said to Tawnya before turning to Mathias. "And I want you to stay out of it. Remember our talk in the cafeteria?"

Mathias nodded once and stepped back, leaving me to face Tawnya's obvious discomfort.

"It's not safe, Mairin. This is for your safety."

I threw up my hands. "You're kidding, right? Aren't you the one who always encouraged me to go out, to spend time with people from school? Now, all of a sudden it isn't safe for me to go to a school event I've attended every year since I started high school? There wasn't a problem before? What changed?"

Tawny looked at my mom and then at Mathias. "Loraine..."

"No, Tawnya. I told you earlier that what you saw wasn't something I agreed with," my mom said. "Mairin, honey, of course you can go to the school tonight."

"Loraine, it's not a good idea," Tawnya said. I noticed her halo was beginning to pulse. Her eyes were wide and she looked more stern than I'd ever seen her. A chill chased down my spine and I took a step back.

"I decide what's good for my daughters, Tawnya," Mom said flinching slightly when Tawnya's eyes shone with hurt. "Mathias, you'll have Mairin home before midnight, yes?"

"Of course, Ms. Cote."

"Then it's settled."

Tawnya gave my mom a look that said it was anything but settled before she stomped into the reading room. It was only when she'd gone that I realized I'd been holding my breath.

Mom watched her go and I felt guilt flood over me. "I'm sorry, Mom. I didn't meant to..."

"You didn't do anything wrong, Mairin." She hugged me and kissed my cheek. "Tawnya did a reading earlier and she's been going on about some dark cloud in your life ever since. I'll talk to her. You go have fun."

Mom headed toward the reading room and I could hear her talking in low tones to Tawnya before Mathias pulled me out the door. I hated to think that I was the reason they would spend the next several hours or days angry with each other. Tawnya and my mom rarely fought, but when they did argue, the fights could be epic. I hoped this one wouldn't drag on too long. Tawnya might convince Mom that Mathias was the problem if she had enough time or ammunition.

"I did not wish to be the source of problems with your family, Mairin."

"You aren't the problem, Mathias," I said. "I am."

"Do you always accept responsibility for what others have done?" Mathias asked.

"I'm not doing that," I said, but I knew he was right.

"Always so concerned with the happiness of others," he said. "Surely I don't deserve you."

"I'm not a saint, Mathias. I'm actually pretty selfish. I didn't want Tawnya to convince Mom that I shouldn't be with...go with you tonight, so I picked a fight with her. Now she and Mom will be upset with each other and it's my fault."

"If you would prefer not to go tonight, I will certainly understand."

I blinked slowly, stunned by the pain that bloomed in my gut at the thought of staying home. "Do you want me to stay home?"

"Of course not," he said, leaning against the side of his car. "But you always have the choice to do as you please when you are with me, Mairin. I won't ever force you."

"You're not forcing me," I said softly.

"Then I will pick you up at seven." The sunny smile I adored stretched his lips and I remembered the interrupted moment in the hall.

I straddled Mathias' legs, leaning against his chest and pinning him against his car. He stiffened, putting his hands on my shoulders, and pushed me gently away. I ignored him and cupped his face in my palm.

"Mairin, this is unseemly," he whispered. I heard an edge of desire in his voice and it made me bold to realize he wasn't as reserved as he wanted me to believe.

"What if I don't care?"

He sighed, turning his face to kiss my palm before straightening up and carefully pushing me away.

"I care about you and your reputation, Mairin, even if you don't."

The hot, choking tears surprised me. I fought them back, turning away so he wouldn't see how hurt I was. It was a weak excuse at best for not wanting to touch me, to kiss me, on my terms.

"No, my sun," he said, lifting my chin to stare into my eyes. "Never doubt that every touch from you is welcome. I simply will not allow myself to endanger you in any way. That includes your reputation."

"Why do you care about my reputation so much? It's not like one kiss would destroy me."

Pain creased his forehead. He leaned down, brushing his lips against my forehead.

"I will see you in a few hours."

He slipped into his car and was gone before my stunned and numb brain deciphered the whispered words that had accompanied his kiss.

"It would destroy us both."

***

The football stadium was already brimming with students and parents when Mathias pulled his car into the student lot. I huddled into the passenger seat, attempting to disappear as people stared into the darkened windows. I was pretty sure no one could see me, but I'd have to get out of the car eventually.

The hours waiting for Mathias to come to pick me up had been excruciating. I'd vacillated between cursing and crying for the majority of the time as I alternated between being angered by Mathias' rebuff and being crushed by it. I hadn't been until almost six thirty that I realized this first date with Mathias would have an audience. Most of the town would be there and they would all be inordinately interested in the new resident and his choice of date. I was in full panic mode by the time Mathias knocked on the door.

"You are lovely, Mairin," he said, kissing my hand.

"Thanks," I mumbled.

"Shall we go?" He glanced past me to the stairs Kerry had just run up.

I sighed. There was no turning back. "Yeah, I guess I can only die of embarrassment once."

Mathias looked at me strangely, but took my hand and led me to his car.

Now we were surrounded by nearly every Highland Home resident and I couldn't bring myself to open the door and expose myself to their ridicule and speculation.

"They're going to see you in a moment, Mairin."

"Yeah, I know." I sat up straighter.

"We do not have to stay, you know. We could do something else."

"No, we can't now. Everyone's seen your car. Let's get this over with," I said.

We'd driven mostly in silence. Mathias focused on the road while I focused on what I was going to do when I got home later. When Mathias had arrived at my house pick me up, Kerry had been running upstairs in tears. It seemed my little sister agreed with Tawnya about Mathias. She wanted me to stay away from him.

I was baffled. No one else seemed to have such a strong reaction to Mathias and neither Kerry nor Tawnya would tell me exactly what it was about him that made them want me to stay away. Without a solid explanation, I wasn't going to stop seeing Mathias. I was already lost when it came to the boy who now held my car door open and offered me his hand to help me out of his car.

"Stop worrying," he said. "We're going to have fun tonight."

"Sure, sure. Fun."

Mathias laughed. "Only you could make fun sound like a death sentence, Mairin."

Just as I was going to snap off some smart retort, I realized everyone in the parking lot was staring at us. "Oh my God," I whispered.

"Ignore them. I do."

"It's easy for you. You don't know them like I do."

"Nor do I care to. It is just you and me, Mairin. No one else matters tonight."

We walked through the gate that led out to the field, surrounded by our classmates and their families. Some stared, others made an effort to not look at us at all. I guess my transparency and Mathias' vivid presence made it difficult for people to decide how to handle us.

"Look at that," someone said loudly. "Isn't that the new guy and Mairin Cote? I thought for sure she was a dyke like her mother."

Nothing ever changed, I thought. No matter what, I was still the freak with the lesbian mother. Shame washed over me for thinking of my mother and Tawnya like that. With the color flooding my face, I was certain I was glowing brighter than the stadium lights.

"Only you and me, Mairin." His smooth voice and electric touch kept me grounded.

I nodded, clutching Mathias' hand. I could do this. Cecelia waved at me from the bottom row of seats. Her bright smile helped me take my next breath. As we headed toward my best friend, I saw something that made me wish for invisibility more than I had ever wished for anything in my life.

"Oh crap," I muttered, trying to pull Mathias away from the group of football players gathered near the edge of the field. In the middle of the pack was Braden Lambert, the Highland Home quarterback and Stephanie's boyfriend. I noticed that the muddy green halo around Braden's head and shoulders was even darker than it had been earlier that day. The color was horribly sinister, as though it reflected something more than Braden's normally nasty personality.

My heart thumped heavily and a headache began behind my eyes. I didn't know what to do to stop what would surely be an ugly confrontation.

"Hey freak," Braden shouted. "I've got a bone to pick with you."

For one horrifying moment, I thought Braden was talking to me. Then Mathias paused and stepped in front of me, blocking Braden from my sight.

"I will be happy to discuss your issue at a later time," Mathias said, sizing up the school quarterback. "I am otherwise engaged right now."

Braden blinked slowly as though confused by Mathias' formality. "I don't care what you're doing, freak. You owe my girl an apology and I plan to take it out of your ass."

"I will not fight with you," Mathias said calmly. He looked down at me. "Mairin, will you please stop tugging on my arm?"

I stopped my attempt to physically restrain him and stepped closer to Mathias. Maybe I could diffuse the situation if I apologized. "We're sorry," I said.

"No, we are not," Mathias said. "Your girlfriend was deliberately cruel to Mairin. I did nothing but elicit an apology from her."

"From what I hear, you did a lot more than that. You're gonna pay for scaring my girl, freak."

"I don't think so. I told you, I will not fight you. Now is not the time or place for this."

I looked around and realized everyone was watching the exchange between Braden and Mathias. I cringed. If they started fighting now, the rest of the team would jump in on Braden's side. I doubted if any of the spectators would take up for Mathias. He was still an outsider in Highland Home, especially as he had spurned the opportunity to join the Golden Ones in favor of being with me and my friends. As I surveyed the crowd, I realized that most of the East Hampton football team was paying just as much attention to the confrontation as the Highland Home players. One of the East Hampton players, a tall boy with pale, luminescent green eyes and a vibrant orange halo, stared intently at Mathias. As I watched, he lifted his head and sniffed the air. The movement reminded me of a predator scenting the air for his prey. It was something I never wanted to see again even thought the movement wasn't particularly threatening. A chill ran down my spine and I stepped even closer to Mathias. There was a definite threat implied in the gaze of the East Hampton player. If this situation exploded, Mathias would be alone. I refused to consider the possibility of anyone harming him as I braced myself for what seemed like and unavoidable battle.

I looked away from the East Hampton players, and saw, with relief, that the Highland Home football coach was pushing his way through the crowd. He eyed Braden and Mathias as though they were gladiators about to clash.

"Okay boys, break this up," he said. "Braden, you need to get back with the team."

Braden grinned at Mathias, though it really looked to me like he bared his teeth. It was a chilling look, one I hoped never to see again.

"This isn't over, freak," Braden said. "Not by a long shot."

Mathias bowed slightly, little more than a tipping of his head. The movement reminded me of the old movies where one man challenged another to a duel over the honor of his lady. The movement was enough to open up my line of sight to the East Hampton side of the field and I locked eyes with the pale-eyed boy. He nodded once, much as Mathias had done and turned back to his teammates. I suddenly wanted to get away from the stadium more than anything. I'd had enough weirdness for one day. Two boys, two different but equally threatening halos. Two obvious battle challenges. It was too much.

"Let's go. Please, Mathias," I said.

Mathias continued to watch Braden until the other boy was a safe distance away from us. Only then did he look at me.

"Of course. Your wish is my command."

When it became clear there would be no blood bath, the crowd quickly lost interest, thinning until only a few people stood near us. I took a deep breath and attempted to get a better handle on myself. The strange behavior of the East Hampton player, and the open hostility between Braden and Mathias left me shaken.

"Do you want to go home?"

Mathias' voice broke through my jumbled thoughts. "No, I don't want to go home," I said.

I realized I was shaking when Mathias took my hand and pulled me into his arms. It was the first time he'd allowed himself to touch more than my hand or face and I sighed. I realized the warm earthy scent I'd smelled the first day I'd met him was the scent of his skin and I wanted to lose myself in it.

"You were never in any danger, Mairin," he whispered into my hair.

"I know, but you were."

He laughed. "No I wasn't."

I looked up at him. Had he not seen the other players or the boy from East Hampton? Had he missed Braden's size or vicious nature? "You don't know Braden. He's an animal. He got cited last year for unnecessary roughness after a player from another school wound up in a coma. Braden hit him so hard, the boy didn't wake up for weeks."

"I am sure that was a horrible experience for all involved. But you can rest assured that I was never in any danger from that boy."

"And what about the guy from the other team? He looked at you like you were something he intended to eat for dinner."

"What guy?" Mathias asked, scanning the crowd.

I pointed, "That one. The boy with the brown hair talking to the East Hampton coach."

Shari Richardson | 57

Mathias watched the boy for a few moments before the East Hampton player looked up. The two boys stared hard at each other from across the field before they both turned away. I felt like I had missed a secret handshake or something. Mathias and the other boy had decided something, I was sure of it, but I had no idea what had been decided. I hated feeling out of the loop, but I didn't know how to bring it up without sharing more about myself than I was comfortable doing.

Mathias rubbed my back until I stopped trembling. Leaning against Mathias was like laying down in a rushing stream. His skin was cool against my own overheated body and the electrical current that jumped between us was oddly pleasant. I sighed again.

"Shall we stay or would you rather go somewhere else?" he asked.

"Can we go somewhere else? I think I've had enough teenage posturing and testosterone for one night."

"Would you care to walk with me on the beach?"

I nodded and let Mathias lead me out of the stadium. The car ride was quick and silent. I barely noticed when we passed the public beach access my family had always used. I was too busy running over the confrontation in the stadium to really pay attention to where we were going. Mathias turned off the car at the end of a long driveway. I looked out at the crashing waves, entranced by the beauty of the moonlit night.

"Where are we?" I asked.

"My home," he said. "I hope you don't mind. This stretch of beach is my favorite in this area. It's why I bought this house, actually."

"You have your own beach," I said. "Of course you do."

Mathias took my hand and walked toward the rushing waves. His thumb rubbed restlessly against my hand. He was silent but I could tell he wanted to say something. I wanted to know what it was, but I was afraid to push him to reveal his thoughts. What if tonight had been enough to convince him that I wasn't worth it? Surely he could see how much easier it would be to leave me behind and join the Golden Ones.

Mathias stopped walking, turning to watch the waves break and rush up the beach toward us.

"I realize there are many things about me which make you uncomfortable," he said. "My wealth is only one of those things. I wish I could remove everything about myself that makes you wary of me." He sat in the sand, pulling me down beside him. "Would you be more comfortable with me if I were poor?"

"Probably not," I admitted. Especially since it wasn't his money that made me uncomfortable.

"I am not trying to flaunt my wealth. I just want to share what I have with you."

"You make that sound so much more permanent than a moonlit walk on the beach." I clapped a hand over my mouth. What was it about Mathias that put my filter in a permanent off position?

"How do you always hear what I think?" he mused. "You're right, of course. I do want to share more than a moonlit walk with you, but I also do not wish to frighten you."

"You don't scare me."

He looked at me a moment before he said, "I wish I did."

"Why?" The moonlight was pale against Mathias' raven wing hair and I wanted nothing more than to slip my fingers into his hair and drag his lips to mine. Talk about teenage posturing and hormones run amok.

Mathias sighed. "Perhaps if you feared me, I could be stronger. Your trust in me and of me may yet be the death of us both." He continued to watch the waves. "Tawnya was probably right this afternoon. I am very likely the dark cloud in your life. You should listen to your family and beware of me."

"No, I don't believe that."

"Perhaps you should. I am not as refined as you seem to believe I am, Mairin. There are desires in me that would send you screaming into the night."

"I don't believe you," I said, forcing back images from my dreams.

"I have told you I am selfish, but the worst of my selfishness is that it puts those I care about in danger while the very nature of what I am draws them ever closer to me. I am...there is evil in that level of selfish desire."

"Mathias, you are probably the least selfish person I've ever known."

A deep sadness settled into Mathias' eyes. "You have far too much faith in me, Mairin, but I find I am unable to leave you alone. It is my nature that I've always gotten what I wanted with very little effort or resistance."

"Do you want me to leave you? To resist you?" My heart hammered unhappily in my chest. The thought of leaving him now was something I wasn't willing to entertain. I needed Mathias in a way I never believed I would need anyone. Especially not an impossibly gorgeous, wonderfully mysterious boy who was way out of my league. I held my breath as Mathias considered my question.

"No," he said softly. "I don't want that."

"Then what do you want?"

He lifted his hand and lay it against my cheek. "I want you."

I mirrored his movements, laying my hand against his cheek. "I want you too," I said.

He leaned down and brushed his lips against my forehead before trailing them down my cheek to my neck. My heart jerked into a swift rhythm and I gasped. Each touch of his lips was both cold and electric, far more intense than when we touched hands.

"Mairin," he whispered. "My heart, my sun. What is this that you do to me?"

My hormone-numbed brain snapped into crystal clear focus. I had heard Mathias speak those words before. To Kathryn. He had kissed Kathryn. She had kissed him as well.

I struggled to reach his lips, desperate for my first real kiss to be from this amazing, beautiful and mysterious boy. Instead of pulling me closer and bringing his lips to mine, Mathias sighed.

"No, my heart," he said, and leaned back. He stood, brushing the sand from his pants

"What?" My heart stopped and then fell. He didn't want to kiss me.

"Not yet. Perhaps not ever. I cannot be that selfish." he said, reaching down to help me up.

I stared at him in stunned silence. Never kiss me? Had he really said he might never kiss me? Mathias took my hand and started walking again. My emotional roller coaster continued to run at full speed. I was angry and hurt and not just a little overwhelmed by the night. I tried to hold on to one emotion at a time, to give myself enough focus to talk to him, to tell him how much it hurt to think of never kissing him. To help him understand that I wasn't easy, that I'd never been kissed and that I was ready to have that wonderful and mythical first kiss, but only if it came from him. Finally, it was anger that settled me down and gave me my voice.

"What just happened?" I demanded.

"Nothing happened, Mairin. That was the point."

"You are the most infuriating person I've ever met," I spat. How could he be so calm while I was in such turmoil?

"I believe you," he said, smiling.

I ground my teeth. I didn't understand what was going on. I was confused and hurt and humiliated.

"I think I should go home."

"Certainly," Mathias said, turning and walking me back toward his car.

Mathias' reasonable attitude made me want to scream. Well, scream wasn't all I wanted to do. If I was honest with myself, I wanted to push him down in the sand and kiss him until neither of us could breathe. The fact that he didn't share this particular compulsion made me ache.

He held the car door for me and chuckled softly when I threw myself into the seat. "So impatient," he said, kneeling beside the car so ours eyes met. "Will you forgive me if I tell you I refrain from kissing you only at great cost?"

"Maybe."

He brushed his lips over my cheek, raising chills along my spine. "You cannot imagine the restraint I must call upon to refrain from taking your lips and devouring them as one might devour a ripe fruit. I want to taste you in so many ways, but I know I cannot. Forgive me now, Mairin, I beg you. What I do now, or refrain from doing, is for your own good."

"I'd rather decide for myself what's for my own good," I said, turning my lips toward his. He smiled, but stepped back.

"When you have all the facts, Mairin, you can decide for yourself. Until then, please trust me."

I crossed my arms and huffed, knowing I looked like an idiot but unable to stop myself.

Mathias was silent as we made our way back to my house. I watched him, marveling at the smooth way he moved and grinding my teeth in frustration. He'd said I could make my decisions when I had all the facts, but he seemed disinclined to share those facts with me. I was getting more annoyed by the minute, but something kept me from questioning him. I was a coward, I decided. I feared that his explanation would separate us somehow.

The lights were on in the kitchen when Mathias pulled up to my house. I wondered if my mom or Tawnya waited for me. Either way, I knew I didn't want to talk to anyone about tonight or about Mathias. What could I say? "Yeah, I think I'm in love with a guy I dreamed of before I met, but he doesn't want to kiss me because he says he's no good for me." That was definitely not a discussion I wanted to have tonight.

Mathias turned in his seat and trailed his fingers along my jaw. I trembled, excitement blooming in my body from each place our skin touched.

"May I call you tomorrow, Mairin?"

His beautiful face filled my vision and I wanted to find the strength to tell him no, to find a way to get some distance and perspective, but I couldn't. I wanted to be with him, near him, a part of him. I wouldn't...no, couldn't...distance myself now.

"Sure. Anytime," I said.

Mathias took my hand and kissed the back of it. My pulse raced and I had to restrain myself from reaching for him. "I look forward to it," he said.

I closed the car door with a little more force than was strictly necessary and flushed when I heard him laugh. I stomped up the walk, refusing to turn and see his amusement.

Chapter 5

"Mairin, will you sit and talk with me?" Tawnya asked after I closed the door behind me.

"I'm kind of tired, Tawnya. Can this wait until tomorrow?"

"I don't think it can, honey. Please sit down."

Something in her voice stopped me. Tawnya rarely used pet names like "honey" for anyone other than my mom. She was obviously upset. Despite my own confusion and fatigue, I decided that I needed to find out what Tawnya thought was wrong with Mathias. I took the chair across from her and waited.

Tawnya toyed with the sugar bowl for a few moments before she sighed and looked across the table at me.

"Tawnya, you're kind of creeping me out," I said. "What's going on?"

"You know how much I love you and Kerry and Loraine, right Mairin?"

"Sure."

"And you know that I would never let any of you get hurt. Not if there was any way to avoid it."

Fear curled deep in my stomach. "What are you trying to tell me, Tawnya?"

Tawnya stared at her hands. "Those halos you've started seeing, I'm pretty sure they're auras, not halos. Well, most of them aren't halos. When you said you saw gold around my head this morning, you startled me. No one else has ever seen what you can see around me."

"I was going to ask you about those halos...er, auras actually. I noticed there are a few different colors I can see, though most everyone has some variation of blue. Why are there different colors? What do the colors mean?"

"Well I can answer why my aura is different from your mother and your sister. As to any others, we'll have to research them. But that isn't really what I wanted to talk about."

Tawnya's gaze flickered toward the door. I knew she'd heard the heavy growl of the powerful engine in Mathias' car. She'd probably heard me slam the car door as well. My anger with Mathias and confusion over his distance lingered and I turned it on Tawnya.

"Please don't start in on Mathias again, Tawnya. Mom already told you she didn't believe the reading you did. If she doesn't believe it, why should I?"

"You need to know what I know, Mairin. Before it's too late." Tawnya rose and paced the length of the kitchen. "When I saw the dark influence in the cards, I didn't know you'd already met him. I thought the shadow was still on the horizon. But when you brought him to the shop, brought him near your mother and your sister, I knew I had to keep you away from him. He's dangerous, Mairin. Dangerous in ways you haven't imagined or dreamed of in your worst night terrors."

I shook my head, but the fear continued to bloom in my gut. Tawnya didn't know about the dreams I'd had of Mathias. She couldn't. I hadn't told anyone but Cecelia about the killing, the blood.

"You're wrong about him. He's good and decent. Certainly better than any of the boys from around here." I said, ignoring the deep, nauseating fear that settled deep into my gut. "He wouldn't even kiss me tonight. How could he be dangerous?"

"There are many kinds of danger, Mairin."

Tawnya crossed her arms across her chest, hugging herself. She took a deep breath before she spoke again. I could see she was struggling with whether to tell me something or not and I was suddenly more afraid of her than I believed I could ever be of Mathias. Something deep inside told me that some part of my past was about to come crashing down on me, taking my future with it.

"Mairin, do you remember the first time you met me?"

The question surprised me. "I don't think so. I just remember you were there at Daddy's funeral."

"You were so tiny the first time I saw you," she said. "I've watched you grow and I've loved you as if you were my own. I loved you because I loved your mother, but also because of who…what you are."

"I don't understand. What do you mean, 'what I am?'"

Tawnya waved me off, continuing her tale in her way. "I've been with you since before you were born. I was supposed to leave you with Loraine and Dick and go back to Heaven, but I couldn't. I couldn't leave you. I knew you were going to be a most extraordinary child…woman…and that you would need my help. And then I fell in love with Loraine and I knew I couldn't ever leave. I gave up my wings to stay here with you, your mother and your sister. I've never regretted a moment of my time here. How could I regret the love I have because of that decision?"

"You were supposed to go back to Heaven?" The room tilted as what Tawnya was saying sank into my over stressed brain. "You're an angel?"

"Not anymore," she said with a small smile. "When I return to Heaven, after you and your mother and sister have lived your lives, I'll be an angel again."

"And that's why your aura is gold, isn't it?"

"Yes."

Tawnya let me digest what she'd said, watching me closely. I could tell by her expression she believed I would freak out at any moment, but actually what she said made an awful lot of sense. The day of my father's accident, he was supposed to be taking me and Kerry to a dentist appointment, but Tawnya kept us home. She was in every memory I had of childhood and she never changed. She took my dreams and now my ability to see auras as a given rather than a curse or an indication that I was strange or freakish. In all, her acceptance of weird was definitely on the high side. It made sense that she accepted the weird things that filled our lives because she was one of those weird things.

"What does any of this have to do with Mathias?" I asked finally. I was determined to get to the bottom of her issues with him. I could deal with Tawnya the angel later. It wasn't like knowing what she was really changed anything between us.

"I can see what he is, Mairin." she said with a deep sigh. "The undead can't hide from the beloved of God."

My jaw dropped and I sat back hard enough that my chair rocked. "The what?" I gasped.

"He's not human. Not anymore at least." Tawnya sat down next to me, taking my hand and pleading with me. "That's why you have to stay away from him."

I felt the tremors begin deep in my gut and spread over my whole body. I was trembling from head to toe when Tawnya reached over and hugged me hard.

"He's not human." I said. "What do you mean by 'not human?'"

"I'm not entirely certain, but I believe he's a vampire," Tawnya said, rocking me slightly in her arms. Her calm voice set the tremors in motion again. How had Tawnya reached into my subconscious and pulled out the single most terrifying possibility of Mathias' existence that lurked there? How could she sit here, so calmly, and tell me that this wonderful boy who had turned my life upside down was a vampire? How had she known what I'd dreamed?

"Why aren't you certain?" I asked, clutching at the last straws of doubt which would allow me to keep Mathias in my life.

"He was with you in the daytime, Mairin. That's usually a pretty good indication that someone isn't a vampire, but there's something about Mathias that...I don't know how to explain it other than by saying his energy tastes like the vampires I've encountered in the past."

"And how many have you met?" It startled me to realize that if what Tawnya said was true there might be more vampires in the world. Sure I'd read about vampires in novels since I was a kid, but I'd never thought of them as part of my reality.

"Seven over the millenia. There are more here on earth than those I've met, but most shy away from me. They can sense that I'm angelic and most don't want to get that close to an angel. Didn't you notice how he didn't shake my hand today in the shop?"

I had noticed that Mathias seemed unwilling to touch anyone but me, but I'd passed it off as a personality quirk. Surely he hadn't avoided touching Tawnya because he knew she was an angel. But he hadn't offered his hand to my mother either, I realized. And when Stephanie had touched him in the cafeteria, he'd jerked away from her. He only seemed to want physical contact with me, and then only on a limited basis and on his own terms.

"Why would a...Mathias be unwilling to touch people in general?"

"I don't really know, Mairin. I think most people would be uncomfortable touching a vampire. They'd know the creature wasn't human, even if they weren't sure why they didn't like it."

"Don't call Mathias a creature," I snapped. "You don't know him and I don't believe he's a...well what you say he is."

"Vampire, Mairin. He's a vampire. The sooner you accept the truth, the easier it will be to walk away from him."

Of course Tawnya couldn't know that I wasn't going to be able to walk away from Mathias. He was already entrenched so deeply into my soul that to remove him would be to remove something vital and necessary for my survival.

I struggled to sit up and Tawnya released me. She watched me as though waiting for me to have hysterics. I knew that wouldn't happen, at least not yet. I was getting used to weird, but this was simply too much for me to deal with. I could feel my brain shutting down. Tawnya's guesses about Mathias were too close to home, too close to my own nightmares for me to accept.

Then, like the light of dawn chasing back the terrors of the night, understanding blossomed. Tawnya couldn't be right about Mathias and I knew why.

"You have to be wrong about Mathias," I said. "His aura is gold, too."

Tawnya's eyes widened. "That can't be."

"But it is. It's not the same color as yours, but it's definitely gold. And like you said, he walks around in the sunlight without bursting into flames. He can't be a..." I swallowed hard and then forced the word past my lips. "vampire."

"It doesn't matter what color his aura is or that he seems to have figured out how to walk in the daylight. What matters is that he's dangerous, Mairin. I want you to promise me that you'll stay away from him," Tawnya pleaded with me. "I don't want to lose you. Think of what it would do to your mother, to Kerry."

"Mathias won't hurt me," I said, though I couldn't say it with any conviction. Mathias had warned me earlier that he was dangerous, that I was putting myself in danger when I was with him. Was it really a good idea to doubt him when Tawnya was confirming his statements?

"He is a vampire, Mairin. No matter what you think are the reasons why he can't be, he can't change what he is. He's a killer. A blood drinker. Every moment you spend with him brings you closer to your death."

"I don't believe you," I said, shuddering. Hadn't Mathias hinted at that very thing earlier? I shoved away from the table. "I don't believe you and I won't stay away from Mathias. For once in my life there is a wonderful person who wants to be with me, no matter what the rest of this little town thinks of me and my family. I won't give that up because you're afraid he might be a vampire. It's ridiculous and I won't promise you anything."

"Please, Mairin. Be reasonable. Think of your mother and sister. What will happen to them if he kills you? Or worse, if he turns you into what he is?"

"I'm going to bed," I said, turning my back on her. "This is a ridiculous conversation and I'm not going to let you twist your fear into my reality. Mom doesn't think Mathias is dangerous. She says I can see him. You can't stop me from seeing him."

Tawnya looked as though I'd slapped her. She stood, her hand reaching out to me and tears building in her eyes. I couldn't remember having ever seen her cry before. Something inside my chest cracked a little and I felt my conviction that I was right and she was wrong slip. But she had to be wrong, I rationalized. Mathias was not a vampire.

I turned and stormed up the stairs to my bedroom, slowing only when I realized I'd wake my mom and Kerry if I kept up with my tantrum. I closed the door to my room and sank onto my bed, dropping my head into my hands. Tawnya couldn't be right. Mathias wasn't a monster. He wasn't a vampire. But there were doubts lingering in my mind even as I argued against Tawnya's revelation.

Mathias had told me himself that he was dangerous. He'd tried to warn me away from him. He wouldn't kiss me. Stephanie was terrified of him. Braden was more than a little interested in fighting him. Was it possible that Tawnya was right? And what about Tawnya? Was she really a former angel staying on earth with a human family, or was that just new age junk? Deep down, I knew I believed Tawnya was a former angel. It really did explain a lot of how she came to be part of our lives and why our lives were as sedate as they were despite the tragedies early on. If I believed she was an angel, why would I doubt what she said about Mathias?

I knew the answer to that question was simple enough. I was in love with Mathias. It didn't matter that I'd only known him for a few weeks. I knew I would never meet another boy, or man, who would take his place in my heart. It wasn't rational, but when was love rational?

"Why is everything in my life so complicated?" I mused aloud.

***

I could see Mathias even in the deep black night that surrounded him. He was pale and luminescent like the moon.

"Come to me, Mairin."

I walked toward him, but in the way of dreams I never got any closer. My steps continued, but he remained out of reach.

"Do you love me, Mairin?"

"You know I do."

"Will you stay with me forever?"

"Yes."

He was beside me then, taking my hand and pulling me close. His lips brushed mine before traveling down to the hollow between my neck and my shoulder. The pain was sharp and sweet. I screamed.

***

"Mairin, wake up. Honey, please."

Mom's voice cut through the dream and pulled me back to reality, but the trip was slow and confused. I opened my eyes, blinking in the bright light.

"Mom?"

"Oh baby, you've been screaming and I couldn't wake you. What were you dreaming?" I saw the fear in her eyes and the lie fell from my lips without hesitation.

"It was nothing, Mom. Same as the last one."

I could tell she didn't believe me, but for once she didn't press for details. I wondered what she and Tawnya had talked about while I had been with Mathias. Had Tawnya shared her theory with my mom? Did Mom believe her?

"Are you okay now?" she asked.

"Yeah, I'm fine. You should go back to bed. You have a big day tomorrow with the charity gig at the country club."

"Are you sure?" I could tell she was battling with herself between letting the lie stand and making me tell her what I'd dreamed.

I hugged her hard. "I'm sure. It wasn't a premonition, Mom. I promise." That much was true at least. It couldn't be a premonition because if it were, it would mean Mathias really was a vampire. I simply couldn't accept that.

She looked at me for a moment before she stood. "Will you try to sleep some more tonight?"

"Of course, Mom. I'll go right back to sleep."

"Okay." She kissed me before leaving and closing the door behind her.

I clutched my knees and rocked back and forth. I could still feel the pressure of Mathias' teeth in my shoulder. I was afraid to get up and look in the mirror. Afraid there would be teeth marks.

My dreams were rarely as vivid as the one I'd just had without being prophetic. I didn't want to believe this one foretold my future in any way. If I believed in the future of the dream, I had to believe in the reality of Mathias as a vampire. I wasn't ready to do that without talking to him.

I realized I didn't have Mathias' phone number. I had no way of reaching him without simply showing up on his doorstep, and I wasn't willing to do that in the middle of the night. Not if he was a vampire. Even if he wasn't, I couldn't just show up and expect him to talk to me about Tawnya's suspicions and my dream. I'd simply have to wait for him to call me, as he'd promised to do when he'd dropped me off.

"Maire, can I come in?" Kerry called from outside my bedroom door.

"Sure." I moved over and made room on the bed for Kerry to sit down.

"It was a bad one tonight, wasn't it?"

I nodded. "I'm sorry I woke you, sis."

"I wasn't sleeping anyway. I heard what Tawnya told you when you got home tonight. I've been thinking about it and wondering how to convince you that she's right."

"Please don't you start on that kick now," I said. "There is no way I'm going to believe the worst of Mathias. Worse than the worst even. He's a good person, Kerr. I know he is."

"Mairin. I'm begging you. Please don't go anywhere with him alone. I don't want to lose you. I don't think I could stand to lose you."

"You're not going to lose me, Kerry. Mathias won't hurt me."

"You don't know that."

"And neither you nor Tawnya know that he will hurt me. You're overreacting."

"And you're rationalizing."

We looked at each other, each certain the other was wrong, dead wrong. I broke the silence when I couldn't stand the pain in her face any longer.

"I'll be safe, Kerry. I promise to be around long enough to annoy your grandchildren."

I hugged her and pushed her off the bed. "Go back to bed, Kerry. Try to get some sleep."

She stood next to my bed, watching me with an intensity that made me wonder what gifts she might be developing. "I love you, sis," she said.

"I love you too."

When she left, I curled up on my bed, hugging my pillow. I could feel the dream lying in wait at the edges of my consciousness, waiting for me to slip back into sleep so the horror could run free again. I fought it, jerking awake several times when I dozed before I succumbed. Finally, Mathias called my name and I went to him. I offered my neck and waited for the pain.

Chapter 6

"Mairin, are you going to stay in bed all day?" Mom said from my bedroom doorway.

I struggled to open my eyes, shocked to realized that I'd slept at all after the dream I'd had the night before.

"What time is it?"

"Almost eleven."

I sat up too quickly and the darkness bloomed across my vision. I never slept half a day away. I rarely slept more than six hours in any given night.

"I'm up, Mom," I said, waving in her direction. "Why are you still here? Don't you have to be at the country club by noon?"

"I wanted to be sure you were OK before I left."

"I'm fine. I guess I needed sleep."

Mom watched me for a moment before speaking. "Tawnya and I will be back late tonight. Can you handle dinner for you and Kerry?"

"Sure, Mom."

"Then have a good day."

When I was sure she wouldn't see me wobble when I stood up, I got up and closed the door before flopping back onto my bed.

There was definitely something wrong with me this morning. I was dizzy and still tired. I felt like I could probably go back to sleep if I closed my eyes. That was definitely not normal for me.

I heard the phone ring and my heart jumped into an erratic rhythm. Mathias had said he'd call me today. Of course it was silly to think he'd know the moment I awoke. Surely it wouldn't be him on the phone now.

"Mairin, phone," Kerry shouted.

My heart leaped into my throat and chills ran down my arms. I snatched the phone from my desk. "Hello?"

"Good morning, Mairin." His voice made me tremble. "I hope you had a pleasant night."

"Morning," I said. "Kerry, I've got it." I waited for the click before I spoke again. "We need to talk, Mathias."

"That sounds ominous," he said. I could hear the teasing note still in his voice.

"Can I come to your house?"

The silence before he answered was thunderous. "That might not be a good idea, Mairin," he said. "Perhaps we could meet at the coffee shop downtown? I feel terrible that I compromised your reputation by taking you to my home last night. I wouldn't want your mother to rescind her permission for my presence in your life."

I smiled at the old fashioned notion of Mathias being able to compromise my reputation by taking me to his home coupled with the fact that he wouldn't even kiss me. Despite the pleasant memories the thought conjured, the fear that had slept as I did curled in my gut again. I had to know if Tawnya's suspicions were accurate. I had to know if I was falling--had fallen already--in love with a vampire. "I don't think this is a conversation you want to have in a public place, Mathias."

He sighed and I could picture the slightly frustrated look he was likely wearing. "Should I come to pick you up or would you prefer to have an escape route?"

His tone stopped me. He sounded resigned and sad, not annoyed. If I hadn't known better, I would have sworn that he knew what I wanted to talk to him about. I could feel a chasm, so like the ones in my dreams, erupt between us, as though he were preparing himself for an inevitable and painful separation because he knew I wouldn't make the leap of faith to be with him. My heart clenched tight and hot in my chest at the thought of a separation. The not knowing was going to kill me, but what would the pain of leaving Mathias do?

"I don't think I'll need an escape route," I said finally, "but I think I'll drive out to your place. No sense in you having to drive in circles."

"As you wish. When should I expect you?"

"Is an hour too soon?"

"Of course not. I look forward to your visit."

"Liar," I whispered. "I'll see you in an hour."

I hung up the phone and dashed to the shower. I was drying my hair when Kerry knocked on my door.

"You're going to him, aren't you?" she said.

"Yes, I'm going to talk to Mathias, Kerry. I want to put this ridiculous thing to rest so we can all move on."

"Promise me you'll come home." Kerry's eyes were wide with fear. After all the years in our family, the oddities of a mother who ran a metaphysical shop, a sister who had visions and an angel who lived under our roof, it broke my heart to know only my association with Mathias had ever put that look of terror and horror in her eyes.

"Of course I'll come home, silly. I'll even stop at the store and get stuff for your favorite dinner."

"I don't care about dinner, Mairin. I care about you."

I hugged Kerry. We'd always been close, but my little sister had never been this emotional around me before. "I promise I will be home tonight to make you dinner, Kerr. Don't worry, please."

I could see she was going to worry no matter what I said, but she nodded and left me alone so I could finish getting ready. I stood in front of the mirror I rarely used and refused to acknowledge that I was taking far more time getting ready than I normally would have because I wanted to look good for Mathias. Better that vanity delay me than the fear of learning the truth.

A little voice kept whispering, "Why bother. He's a vampire and if you live, after today you'll never see him again." I squashed that voice again and again, but it kept returning.

The drive to Mathias' home took me past The Astral Plane. Shock and apprehension stabbed deep as I passed the shop and saw the East Hampton football player from the night before stepping out the door onto the street. He looked up, locking eyes with me as he had at the stadium last night, and then he turned away. My heart lodged somewhere in my throat, and I continued though our quiet town and out the beach road to the house I'd dreamed of visiting since childhood.

Mathias met me at the door to what was the grandest house in Highland Home. As a child I'd always wanted to see what the inside of this house was like. The outside reminded me of some of the homes I saw on television when they did shows about what the stars lived like. The inside was even more breath-taking than I had imagined

"Welcome to my home," Mathias said, bowing slightly as he stepped aside to let me in.

"I always wanted to see the inside of this house," I admitted. "When I was a kid, I used to imagine a prince lived here and that he'd rescue me from...well that he'd rescue me." Leave it to me to blurt out that the prince of my childhood fantasies would always rush to rescue me from monsters. Thankfully, the filter on my words that usually shut down the moment I was near Mathias, was working. I couldn't bring myself to say the word "monster." Not now. What if my prince turned out to be the monster?

"Would you like a tour?"

"No, not now. I think we'd better talk first."

"As you wish. Can I offer you anything to drink?"

Mathias' formal tone made my heart stutter. The chasm between us widened ever more. "Um, sure. Ice water would be great."

The back wall of the house was floor to ceiling glass, giving us an uninterrupted view of the ocean. The rolling waves held my attention while Mathias got my drink. I'd always loved the sound and scent of the ocean. Those things were a couple of the very few advantages to growing up in Highland Home. I sipped my drink a few times, unsure how to begin.

Mathias sat down at the breakfast table and watched the ocean, waiting patiently for me to speak. He was so still, so reserved, my heart broke a little more each time I glanced at him.

"I...I don't know-how to start," I admitted, finally sitting next to him and reaching across the table for his hand.

He slowly drew his hand away from mine, settling it in his lap. "The beginning is usually a good place," he said. His smile was endlessly sad.

I swallowed hard against the lump that rose in my throat. How could I speak the words that would doom me to a life without this boy. Did I really care if what Tawnya said was true? Did it matter that this magnificent boy wasn't human? Would that fact change how I felt about him? My nightmares played in a silent loop, showing me the faces of those who had died beneath Mathias' teeth. Nameless faces of men and women long dead rose up, each begging for their own justice. Sadly I realized I could dismiss them all, save one. Kathryn's wide green eyes stared out of my subconscious, accusing me of being careless with my life by loving the boy whom she too had loved. I knew I was in love with Mathias but if he had taken the life of the woman he loved in his quest for blood, what would stop him from doing the same to me? I had to know the truth or live in fear so long as he stayed with me.

"Tawnya had an interesting theory to share with me when I got home last night."

"I thought she might."

"But it can't be right...her theory. It's too ridiculous."

"Perhaps you should share her theory with me, so I can tell you if it is ridiculous."

I looked at him, sitting so still and stiff, as though bracing himself for a blow and I felt the tears well in my eyes. No matter what, if I said the words waiting on the tip of my tongue, there would be no going back.

"Promise you won't laugh," I said, trying to lighten the mood.

"I'm certain whatever Tawnya told you is no laughing matter, Mairin."

"No, I suppose not," I admitted. "She...Tawnya...thinks you're a vampire."

"And what do you think, Mairin?" When he didn't immediately laugh and deny my accusation, hope trickled out of my soul.

"I think...I think you're the most wonderful person I've ever met."

He smiled sadly. "That isn't all you think," he said. "Ask me, Mairin. Ask me the question that makes your eyes shine with tears."

"Are you?"

"Am I what? You have to say the word or you will never believe my answer."

I took a deep breath and looked into Mathias' eyes. I wished I could drown in the black pools staring back at me. The eyes I had come to love so easily were so blank now, icy and closed to me. What had I done? Realizing I'd already gone too far to turn back, I blurted out, "Are you a vampire, Mathias?"

He never blinked nor shifted his eyes from mine. "Yes."

***

"Mairin, open your eyes, please." Mathias' voice broke through the darkness, calling me back to the light.

"Tell me I dreamed it," I said stupidly.

"I promised I would always endeavor to tell you the truth, Mairin, so I cannot tell that lie."

"Oh God," I moaned. "You really are a...a...."

"A vampire. Yes."

I realized I was cradled against Mathias' chest and that we both sat on the kitchen floor. The cool electric current that jumped between us made me want to cling to him and run away at the same time.

"Were you planning to tell me anytime soon?" I asked.

"Not this soon, no, but I knew eventually I would have to be open with you."

I pushed at his shoulder, struggling to get up. Mathias silently released me, remaining on the floor while I backpedaled to the kitchen table. He rose slowly and backed away from me, his arms outstretched.

"I won't hurt you, Mairin," he said softly. The pain in his voice snapped my head up from my contemplation of the table top. I could see his attempt to be nonthreatening was costing him.

"I know that," I said. "I just need some space. I need to think. I need..."

"Of course." Distance, as icy as it was deep, flooded into his voice.

The ache in my chest blossomed and I clutched the edge of the kitchen table until my arms shook. Why was he always so reasonable when I was emotional? How could he remain so calm when I felt my world shattering around me?

"I don't know what I'm supposed to do now. What do you do when the person you love says, 'Oh by the way, I'm a vampire,'?"

"Most sane people would say goodbye, Mairin. I certainly wouldn't blame you if you did."

"No."

He lifted an eyebrow. "No?"

"No, most sane people would still be passed out on the kitchen floor, not standing here having a perfectly reasonable conversation with you."

His laugh was abrupt and bitter. "Yes, I suppose that is true."

I sat down at the table and watched the waves for a few minutes. Mathias was a vampire. Did that mean every one of the dreams I'd had of the past had been his memories? Could his life really consist of nothing but the hunt and the crushing remorse? And what did this revelation mean for us? My soul still cried out in agony each time I considered leaving Mathias. How could I walk away from a love like this and survive? And would he let me go? Could he let me go? Did he feel for me the depth of love I felt for him? Would it destroy his soul as it would mine to be separated from me? I had too many questions, but no answers. I had to have answers. When I turned to find Mathias, he was sitting next to me.

"At least tell me it's not as bad as all the movies and books make it out to be," I said.

"I wish I could, but I cannot tell that lie either." Mathias lay his hand on the table next to mine, neither close enough to touch nor far enough to discourage me should I want to take it. "There are some very real and horrifying facts of my life which make me a monster, Mairin. I should never have allowed myself to become a part of your life, but I could not resist you once I saw you. Would you care to hear my reasons for staying, for putting you in danger every moment you are with me, or should I see you to your car?"

I thought about his offer. I had so many questions but I was afraid to ask them. "Tell me," I said finally. I tentatively lay my hand over his. Mathias covered my hand with his, sighing heavily.

"I told you I was selfish. That I had never been denied anything I truly wanted. That is the sad truth of my life. I was seventeen in 1922. My family was wealthy in a way that doesn't really translate now. We had everything we could ever want or need, but we worked hard for it all. I was a man poised to get everything I'd ever wanted. My father was turning our shipping company over to me and I was engaged to the most beautiful girl in the county. Her name was Kathryn." I started in surprise. Did this revelation confirm that my dreams were his memories? I shuddered at the thought.

Mathias waited silently, pausing in his tale and reaching to touch my face. "She had lovely red-brown hair and green eyes and she loved me. I loved her, too. Loved her enough to die for her."

"The fiend that changed my world found us walking near the docks. Kathryn often met me at the ship my father was currently unloading so we could walk in the evenings before she had to return to her parents' home. We were to be married only days from my last night as a human."

"I heard the monster coming and shoved Kathryn out of the way as it charged us. Kathryn was able to run as I held it and let it sink its foul teeth into my arm."

I shuddered. I could hear the Mathias from my dream scream, "Kathryn, run. Don't look back, just go!"

Mathias smiled softly, stroking my cheek again. "It drank until I could no longer see anything but a dark tunnel. I saw my own death in that last moment and I welcomed it. I knew Kathryn had escaped. That was all that mattered. And then I heard the watch running down the alley. Kathryn had sent them back for me. Would that she had not, I could have died in that fiend's embrace rather than become what it was. Instead of finishing me, it dropped me and ran, leaving my diseased body behind."

Shari Richardson | 83

My heart was thundering in my chest as I listened to Mathias speak. I could almost hear the watch running on cobble stones and hear Kathryn screaming for him. Screaming for him as I would have screamed had I witnessed the horror he described.

"Kathryn sat with me for the several days during which I lingered at death's door. She refused to believe that the doctors my father sent for could not save me. Perhaps if she had let them lead her away...if she hadn't been there...but she was."

I could see the lovely woman from my dream silently praying for Mathias, mopping his brow, and waiting for him to be well. My mind refused to move past that moment in my dream, to move on to what I knew was the outcome before Mathias spoke the words.

"The moment my eyes opened after my heart finally gave up its battle, I could think of nothing but the scorching thirst that burned my throat. I didn't recognize my Kathryn until she lay still in my arms. Pale, still, and very dead. I ran. Coward that I am, I ran rather than face the rightful punishment for my evil. I hid like the base, cowardly monster that I was until the thirst drove me out."

A sob slipped between my lips. Mathias looked at me, wonder in his eyes. He didn't know that what made me cry out was his own anguished face, the chaste kiss he'd left on Kathryn's lips, the promise he'd made to mourn her for eternity. Such love, so much more than I believed I was capable of, couldn't exist in an evil creature. It couldn't be allowed.

He shook himself, coming back from his past to join me in our present. "For too many years, I wandered the night, hiding in alleys, taking life in order to sustain my own existence. Women flocked to me, walked into the dark with me as though they could not see the evil in my heart. I walked the night and I mourned the sun."

Each word he spoke brought with it the visions of my dreams. I had walked those alleys with him. I had seen the death he brought to those women. I had mourned the sun with him. For the first time in my life, I cursed the gift I had been given. I didn't want his memories, their details sharp and horrible. I wanted to continue to be able to doubt his words so I could stay with him, love him.

"It wasn't until decades later that I met Alfred. It was he who shared the secrets of our existence with me. How home soil allows us to live in the light. How our venom makes more of us. How if I were careful, if I could control myself, I could take blood without killing or turning my donors. It was only with his teaching that I was able to step out of the sewers and return to the human world. But even then, I was still a monster, still a killer."

"I count meeting Alfred as my third birthday," Mathias said. "My first was when my mother brought me to this world, the second when my Kathryn left it."

"And even though I'd found ways to be reborn into the light, the light of my mortal life haunted my every moment. There has been a gaping hole in my chest from the moment I realized what I had done, how my selfishness had taken Kathryn from this world. I vowed I would never be that selfish again, that I would never again allow my desire to live in and be surrounded by the light to endanger someone I loved."

Mathias smiled at me. "But I cannot be anything but what I am."

He held my hand to his lips and watched me so intently and silently that I couldn't bear it any longer.

"What happened to Alfred?" I asked softly to break the silence.

"Alfred and I recently parted ways. He travels extensively and unlike me, he does not seek to live among humans for long periods of time. He wanted to go to Europe and I wanted...I wanted some time alone."

I wondered what Mathias had been about to say he wanted, but before I could ask, he continued.

"Don't worry, Mairin, should he visit, I would insist on his word that he not hunt here. I would protect you and your family from me and mine."

I shuddered. "He...he hunts?"

"He does not hunt as much as he did when we met, but he is, shall we say, less civilized about how he obtains his meals than I am."

My mind wouldn't grasp what Mathias was telling me. He could see my confusion and said, "Let me finish my tale, Mairin and I will answer all of your questions. Do you not want to know why I came to live in Highland Home so recently?"

I nodded, not at all certain I really wanted to know what had brought Mathias into my life but unable to resist drawing out the story he spun. The longer he spoke, the longer I could stay with him. If only he were Scheherazade. A thousand nights could easily be a lifetime with Mathias.

"I was drawn to this little town because I needed to replenish my home soil supply. Without it, I would have to live in the darkness, something I could not abide for long. Living in California I could soak in the sun and pretend to be human, but that lifestyle drained the power from my home soil so quickly. I came to take soil from the garden where my Kathryn lays buried and then I planned to return to California."

It jolted me to realize the cobbled streets upon which Mathias had killed were buried under the asphalt here in Highland Home. He noticed my shock and kissed my hand.

"But then I heard your voice, so clear, so pure, so much like my Kathryn's and that changed everything. You and your family were laughing together, coming off the beach after a day in the sun. I watched you from my Kathryn's grave and for the first time in almost a century, my heart sang. I knew I had to stay, that I had to meet you, to understand how it was that after so long, an insignificant human girl could reawaken my human soul."

"And that is the base, selfish reason I endanger your life. You make me feel whole, Mairin and I'm too self absorbed to let go of that wholeness for your safety...unless you tell me I must leave you. If you tell me to go, I think I can do it, though I must admit I'm not at all certain of that."

I sat, silent and still, trying to digest what Mathias had said. I had so many questions and didn't know where to begin.

"I can see the questions you bite back, Mairin. I've told you the worst of what I am. I have confessed to you what I have held in the secret vault of my heart for nearly a century. Nothing you ask me now can harm me, or you, any more than I have already done. Ask me your questions."

There was only question to which I had to have an answer. Mathias didn't understand how deep my fear of his need for death was because he didn't know I had walked the alleys with him. I needed to know if those midnight plunges into the depths of hell were distant memories or part of his present and future. "Do you, I mean do you have to...to.."

"To kill?" he said, finishing with the word I couldn't utter. Even on his lips, it was a bitter condemnation

"Um, yeah."

"Having to kill and being unable to stop myself are two different issues. There are ways to take blood that do not put the...the donor, for lack of a better term, in danger from my venom, but the blood lust that begins at the first drop on my tongue has often negated any steps I've taken to save those who give me their blood. Alfred has hypothesized that because I still connect so closely with my donors that I cannot separate myself from the blood lust. The taste of human blood is a drug to me, one I cannot live without and one that steals any vestige of humanity I may still posses."

"So you still," I swallowed hard, "Hunt?"

"No, Mairin. I don't need to hunt. There are many humans who find my kind irresistible and who are willing to put their lives in danger to fulfill a fantasy."

"But you still kill your, um, donors?"

"More often than not, I do. It is something I have tried very hard to combat, but I have not had a great deal of success." His voice was cold and emotionless, but I could hear his anguished cries as the Mathias of my dreams mourned each person he had killed.

Chills ran down my spine and I felt myself sliding away from Mathias without a conscious thought that I needed to get away from him. His dark eyes were sad as he sat back, releasing my hand and giving me distance.

"I don't know what to do," I said softly. "You're so calm. You can tell me you kill those who offer you blood without emotion. I need to know you feel something, Mathias."

"I carry with me the memory of every face from every donor on whom I've fed. I see them in their last moment and I hear their screams. It has taken nearly a century of practice to inure myself to them, to the screams, but what wretched slip of soul I may still have is wracked with guilt over each and every one of them. If there were another way, I would do it, but only human blood allows me the shadow of a life I have. If it would mean I could live my life at your side, I would gladly starve in order to refrain from doing something I can see repulses you and is taking you from me even now."

"I wouldn't want you to starve, Mathias."

"But you would not have me feed in the only way I have been able to for a century."

"Not if it means people will die," I said. "There is no other way?"

"No, Mairin. No other way. I have done everything I could think of to suppress the blood lust that rises when I feed and there have been times when I have been successful, but so far nothing I've tried has been a surety. Too many times I remember the taste of the blood and awaken to the dead weight of the donor in my arms."

I shuddered. Mathias was calmly explaining how he murdered people despite attempting to leave them alive. I didn't know what to say or do. Part of my brain screamed, "Run," but the part of my soul I'd already lost to him kept me rooted in place. I couldn't leave until I was certain leaving wouldn't destroy me.

"Tell me what to do, Mathias," I begged. "Tell me how to be OK with that...to be able to live with murder as a part of my daily life and I will happily stay and love you until the end of time."

"You must do as your conscience dictates, Mairin. I am, and can only ever be, who and what I am. I could wish I were not a monster, but wishing will not change my fate...or yours. Though I do not believe I will ever stop loving you, I meant it when I told you that you always may do as you please when you are with me. I would never hurt your or your family. To do so would be to further damn myself to an eternity of pain. But if you wish for me to leave you..." he swallowed hard, pausing to pull in one long breath. "If you wish for me to leave you, I will go."

"That's why you wouldn't kiss me," I said, sudden realization dawning in my foggy brain. "You didn't want to risk infecting me."

"There are many things I would wish to do with you, Mairin. Touching you is a joy I never believed possible. Breathing your scent makes my head spin. Seeing your every thought and emotion as it passes through your eyes is a gift of which I am not worthy. But to taste you, any part of you, is to tempt fate to such an extent that even my selfish heart will not allow. I have never wanted anything in my very long life as much as I want to taste your lips. Even my thirst pales in comparison to that desire, but I will not jeopardize your immortal soul to fulfill my selfish desires."

I leaned back hard in my chair, suddenly aware that as Mathias had spoken, I'd edged closer and closer to him.

"You talk to me, about me, as though I were something more than girl," I whispered.

"You are so very much more than a girl, Mairin. From the moment I heard your voice, you became my heart, my sun, my reason to continue in this existence."

"This is too much," I said. "I don't know where to begin to wrap my head around all of this, Mathias."

"I understand, Mairin. I've had nearly a century to come to terms with what I am. You've had a few hours at best. I have all the time in the world to await your decision."

I looked at him, this boy to whom I had already given my heart, and realized I could not tell him to leave. If he left, he would take a part of my soul with him, a part I could not live without for long. But if he stayed, could I accept that he remained a killer? I didn't know how to reconcile these thoughts into something I could live with, something that wouldn't eventually lead to the destruction of my own humanity.

"Why are you able to restrain yourself with me, but not with your donors?" I asked. "Don't you want to...to drink my blood, too?"

Mathias jerked back as though I'd slapped him. "Don't even think....Mairin, must I say the words for you to understand? I love you. Your death would mean the end of my existence. If I were the cause of it..." He stopped and plunged his hands into his hair, pulling it back so tightly, I could only imagine how much it must have hurt.

"If I were the cause of your death, there would not be a deep enough pit in hell to which what remained of my soul could be banished."

"But why is my death so different from your donors? You said you connect to them. Why isn't that connection enough to keep you from killing them?" I didn't say that I knew he felt guilt over their deaths, that I had seen his anguish. I couldn't understand why that wasn't enough to keep his donors alive.

"I don't know," he roared. He shoved away from the table and stood as far from me as he could. "I don't want to be the monster I am. Especially when I see the fear in your eyes, Mairin. Tell me what would take that fear from you and I will do it. I would make any sacrifice you demanded if it meant I wouldn't lose you."

I was stunned by his passion and his pain. "I need to go home. I have to make dinner for my sister." I knew I was grasping at the mundane to keep my mind from settling on the macabre truth. The man I loved was a killer.

"Will you allow me to drive you home, Mairin? For my own peace, and for your safety?"

"I'm OK to drive," I said, knowing I lied. Mathias considered the lie for a moment before nodding.

"As you wish," he said. I heard the finality of his words and my heart broke further.

"I need time to think, Mathias. I know I'm not rational right now and I have to have distance and time to be able to decide what to do."

"Of course, Mairin. I would not wish for anything more." His voice was so dead it gave me chills.

"There are a lot of things I can live with, I think," I said, grasping for a way to tell him the one thing I was sure I couldn't live with.

"But a killer is not one of them," he said, finishing my thought neatly and finally.

"No," I whispered, tears slipping down my cheeks.

Mathias caught one tear as it lay trembling on my cheek and lifted it to his lips. His eyes closed and his beautiful face broke into an angelic smile. Hesitantly, he leaned into me, brushing my forehead, my cheeks and finally my throat with his lips. The cool feel of his breath jerked a deep sob from my throat and he pulled me into his embrace, rocking me until the tears slowed.

When I could, I pulled away from him slowly. I didn't want to hurt him any more than I already had, but I needed distance. He let me go, though part of me prayed he would hold me longer.

"I have to go," I said.

He walked me to the door and held it open for me.

"Will you..." he stopped. "No, I have no right to ask anything of you."

"What were you going to ask me?"

"Will you allow me to stay in Highland Home for a time? Until I can settle my affairs and move back to California."

I knew that hadn't been his question, but I let the lie pass. "I can't ask you to leave, Mathias. For more reasons than I'm ready to deal with, I can't ask that of you. All I am asking for right now is time and distance. Let me find my path. Don't interfere while I'm searching."

He nodded once and then slowly closed the door between us.

Chapter 7

I sat in the Nova for a long time before the tears slowed enough for me to see. My mind wouldn't let go of the image of Mathias slowly closing the door. It was so final, as though he was more certain of my future than I ever would be. Certain of a future that didn't include him. I tried to imagine that future, but there was only the crushing darkness of my dreams. I could no longer see even the mundane future of college and the career I'd always planned for. It was as though Mathias had closed the door on my entire future, not just the one which included him.

I drove slowly through town, stopping at the grocery store to get the things I needed to make Stromboli for Kerry. Part of me still stood on the threshold of Mathias' house, waiting for him to open the door and laugh; to tell me it was all a terrible joke. He wasn't a vampire. He wasn't a killer. He wasn't a monster. I knew better, but I couldn't let go of the hope.

I stood next to my car, struggling to control my emotions, knowing it was a lost cause. In my entire life, the only time I'd ever had complete control of my emotions had been at Daddy's funeral. I never cried for him where Mom or Kerry could see me. Any other emotional upheaval I'd ever had poured out of me and onto everyone and everything in my life. I knew I couldn't go into the store until I had better control over myself. Too many people would see me and tell Mom or Tawnya. It would be just another scandal for the Cotes. I couldn't let that happen.

"Hey, are you okay?"

I looked up into the pale green eyes of the East Hampton football player who had stared at me and Mathias. I jerked back, startled and more than a little afraid.

"Um, not really, but it's just girl stuff," I said.

The boy held out his hand and I took it reflexively. "I'm Xavier Meyers. I saw you last night at the pep rally."

"Yeah."

"Look, I know you're probably kind of freaked out right now, but I needed to talk to you. Can we maybe sit in your car or something?"

"I don't think that's a good idea."

"Mairin, this isn't a conversation you want to have in public."

The echo of the words I'd spoken to Mathias that morning shook me. The tears began again in earnest leaving Xavier watching me, obviously unsure what to do.

"How...how do you know my name?" I asked when the tears slowed.

"Your mom and my grandmother know each other from the psychic community," Xavier's relief at getting a coherent question out of me despite the tears was obvious. "When I described you to my grandmother, she said you were probably the one I'd seen last night."

I rubbed the tears from my face and eyes. Crying over Mathias wasn't making me feel better and I felt more than a little foolish bawling all over this stranger.

"What did you want to talk about?"

"Really, I think a little privacy would be better for this talk."

"Oh fine," I snapped. "Get in."

Xavier slipped into the passenger seat, turning so his back was against the door and he faced me. I kept staring at his eyes and his pulsing orange aura. The two features were enough to numb my already assaulted brain.

"You kept staring at me last night." I said.

"Yeah. That's why I needed to talk to you." Xavier shifted uncomfortably. "Look, I know what I'm going to tell you is going to make me sound like a lunatic," he coughed out a laugh. "But trust me, it will all make sense when I'm finished. Okay?"

I nodded. It wasn't like I wasn't already overwhelmed by the bizarre. What was one more crazy story?

"OK, so I was staring at you last night because of that guy you were with."

I jerked. Why couldn't I catch a break? Mathias was going to be the death of me. I shuddered at that thought.

"There's something you need to know about that guy. Something that makes him a danger to everyone around him."

"He's a vampire." I said.

It was Xavier's turn to be surprised. "You knew?" Revulsion warred with anger in his tone.

"Not last night, no," I said. "I just came from his house. He...he confirmed what my mom's partner told me last night."

"Then you know how dangerous he is, Mairin. He's a killer."

"I know," I screamed. The vehemence of my response startled me. "I know what he is, Xavier."

Mathias was the boy I loved. He was kind and compassionate. He was a protector of those he cared about and the people they loved.

Mathias was a killer.

The distance between the illusion of Mathias' humanity and the reality of his existence was like a sucker punch to the gut. Bitter laughter burst from my lips, quickly transforming into sobs.

Xavier waited silently for me to get myself under control before he spoke again.

"I have to say I'm surprised he let you leave his lair after you learned the truth."

"It's a house, not a lair," I said.

"Whatever," Xavier snapped. "The point is, most blood suckers would have killed you and destroyed your body. This one didn't."

"What do you want from me? Do you want me to go back so Math...he can kill me?"

"No, no. Of course not. But it does change my plans for him."

"Why would you have plans for...him." I couldn't speak his name. It choked me with the weight of what my life was going to be without him.

"Well let's just say part of my job is to keep the human world safe from blood sucking demons and other nasty creatures. But I can't act if the blood sucker hasn't demonstrated that he's an immediate threat. This one seems to have enough control to allow someone who knows his secret to leave without consequences. I'll have to wait for him to become a bigger threat."

"You're crazy," I said. "You're just a kid. Who appointed you to the post of protector of the human race?"

"It's not a job I wanted, I can tell you that. But I won't walk away from my duty." Xavier's bitter tone reminded me of Mathias' as he'd recounted his tale of becoming a vampire.

"Look, Mairin, I'm sorry to jump on you about this today. Obviously you've had a tough day. But I need to know what you plan to do about the blood sucker now."

"Stop calling him that."

Xavier sighed. "Fine, what would you prefer I call him? Fiend of the night?"

"His name is...Mathias." I pushed his name past the lump in my throat.

"OK. What do you plan to do about Mathias?"

"Why do you care?"

"I'll be watching him. Making sure he doesn't start killing the innocent townsfolk of Highland Home. I need to know if I have to watch out for him turning townsfolk too."

"Turning?"

"Yeah, making more little blood suckers to decimate the human population."

I tried to wrap my brain around what Xavier was suggesting. "You think I'd let him make me into a vampire?"

"Well, it wouldn't be the first time someone thought they were in love with a blood sucker and let them end their human life by making them a hell borne atrocity."

"Big words for a football player," I laughed bitterly.

"Bite me, Mairin," Xavier said. "I really don't care what your decision is. I just need to know how closely I'll need to watch you."

I shook my head. "I don't know what to tell you. I haven't made up my mind about...about him, but I can tell you that I won't be letting him make me a vampire."

"Good enough." Xavier stepped out of the car. "You should just stay away from the blood...from Mathias. Think of what your death would do to your family. And accidents happen."

He was gone before I could think of anything to say.

***

I tried to go back to my life, but I should have known it would be impossible. Meeting Mathias had changed something important in my makeup. I couldn't just walk away unscathed.

I wouldn't talk to anyone about what had happened between me and Mathias. I stopped talking to Tawnya altogether until Mom shouted that she wouldn't let me drive away the woman she loved. After that screaming match, I put on my happy face and hid my true feelings from everyone. I wouldn't even let Kerry in close enough to share my broken heart with her. I still hadn't found a way to make a decision about Mathias and so I left him in the ether with me. Every so often he would look at me, a question in his eyes, but I ran from those moments.

I wanted to find someone to blame for my pain and for Mathias'. The trouble was, I could find no one but myself to foot that bill. I had ignored my dreams and allowed myself to get involved with Mathias because I was dazzled by him. I had gone to him with questions and then blamed him when the answers were what I already knew to be true. I had let him close the door between us because I was too cowardly to stop him.

I didn't tell anyone about the weird meeting with Xavier either. The whole episode seemed distant and unreal, like it had been part of someone else's life. From time to time, I'd see Xavier around Highland Home, but he never acknowledged me or spoke to me.

I tried to avoid seeing Xavier rather than searching for him in Highland Home. To see Xavier was to acknowledge why he was there. To acknowledge that was to allow myself to be forcibly reminded of what Mathias was and how I was letting months pass without making a decision.

Slowly, the painful days and horrifying nights blended into something smooth and easy to ignore. I dreamed of Mathias almost every night. I screamed when his teeth sank into my shoulder. I cried when his lips brushed my forehead. It got so bad that Mom stopped coming to my room when I screamed. I couldn't tell her what I was dreaming and she finally stopped asking. I woke each day wondering what new hell I was in for.

Eventually, though, my soul began to heal itself, even if that healing consisted of only a scab over the festering hole where my heart once lay.

"Want to go with me to the mall later?" Cecelia asked. I realized she'd been talking to me for at least the five minutes it took to get from the cafeteria to French class, but I couldn't remember what she'd said.

"What?"

"Look Mairin," she said, irritation making her voice sharp. "I get it. He was wonderful and all that, but you told him to get lost. You gotta stop moping after a guy you said you didn't want. It's been six months. You have to move on, Chica."

I looked at Cecelia, realizing I hadn't really seen her in months. She'd changed her hair and I hadn't noticed. I wondered what else I'd missed while I wallowed in self-pity. Shame settled deep in the pit of my stomach. "I'm sorry I've been such a terrible friend," I said.

"You're not a terrible friend, doofus. But you're not the same Mairin you were before Mathias. I miss you and I wish you would let me help you feel better. You won't talk to me. You won't let me help you. Mairin, I don't know what to do."

I flinched at his name. I'd spent so many months avoiding anything to do with him, including his name that when something came up, like now, I didn't know how to handle it. I saw fear and worry in my best friend's eyes and felt a drowning guilt. Cecelia was right. I wasn't the same girl I'd been before a vampire had turned my world upside down. I was, at best, a shadow of myself who was hurting everyone she loved. I suddenly realized I was a worse kind of monster than Mathias. At least he killed cleanly. I let my victims suffer and linger.

"Speak of the devil and the devil will appear," I whispered.

Mathias stood at the door to the French classroom, talking to Mr. Petrowski and pointedly not looking at me. I stared at him, drinking in his beloved features, ignoring the pain that bloomed in my chest. As though I were seeing my world clearly for the first time since Mathias had closed the door on me, I realized that he didn't look as I remembered him. He looked paler today than I remembered. In fact, he looked downright ill once I really looked at him.

"Does he look okay to you?" I asked Cecelia.

She didn't have to ask me who I meant. She was game, though and glanced at Mathias. "He looks the same as he always does, Maire."

I nodded distractedly at Cecelia, letting her change the subject but not really letting go of my suspicions. Cecelia wouldn't notice the change in the paleness of Mathias' skin or the darker shadows under his eyes. She hadn't memorized his face when he'd been happy, so she wouldn't see the drastic changes now apparent to me. How long had he looked tired and ill and I'd seen only the face I remembered from my dreams?

Mathias glanced up, his eyes pausing briefly on me before he ducked into the classroom. I knew when I found my seat, he would be as far away from me as he could get. He'd taken my desire for distance truly to heart. He hadn't spoken to me in months, not since I'd screamed at him to give me time a few weeks after we'd spoken at his home.

I could still see the defeated look on Mathias' face from that day.

"I need time, Mathias," I'd screamed.

"Of course, Mairin. I only wished to tell you that I am waiting when you've made your decision."

"When I've decided, You'll be the second to know," I'd snapped.

He'd walked away, blending into the crowd and leaving me to watch him disappear.

From that day on, he'd avoided me. He refused to speak to me and rarely looked at me. We passed each other in the halls, sat through classes together, but we didn't communicate. If in the past several months I had made a decision in which I wanted him as part of my life, his determined efforts to avoid me would have made it impossible for me to tell him.

French was the worst of all the times I was forced to be in the same class with him because our teacher insisted that everyone speak at least once during every class. Mr. Petrowski's policy meant I had to hear Mathias' rough silk voice and try not to flinch too much. Today I couldn't help turning in my seat to find him when I heard him answer Mr. Petrowski in perfectly accented, but extremely softly spoken French. His dark eyes appeared even darker with the heavy shadows beneath them. Not even his pale gold aura could brighten his appearance. Something was definitely wrong.

"So are you up for the mall tonight?" Cecelia whispered when Mr. Petrowski turned his back on us.

"Can't," I said. "Mom is making me sit down with that East Hampton psychic tonight. Something about her being an expert in auras I think."

"Damn. Maybe you'll be done early." Cecelia turned around, narrowly avoiding being caught by Mr. Petrowski.

I could hope the same as Cecelia, but I was almost certain my entire weekend would be packed full of new age silliness. My mother had gotten it into her head that if I understood my new "gift" better, I might snap out of the funk I'd been in all winter. I think only Tawnya really understood what was behind my melancholy, but she was certain that staying away from Mathias was in my best interest. Far from a sympathetic ear, Tawnya was positively gleeful that I had chosen humanity over love.

"Cece, I'll met you at the car," I said as I dashed out of the classroom in pursuit of Mathias.

I knew he heard me running after him, but Mathias refused to slow his steps.

"Mathias, please wait. I need to talk to you."

He froze, a shudder rolling over him. He turned, a decidedly unfriendly look fixed firmly on his beautiful face.

"Mairin." My name had never before sounded like a curse on his lips.

"I..." I didn't know what to say now that he'd stopped and was so openly hostile.

"I have an engagement this evening, Mairin. Did you truly wish to speak with me or were you seeking only to torment me further?"

"I didn't mean to torment you," I said before I could stop myself. I hadn't thought I'd been tormenting him. I knew I'd tormented myself, but apparently my indecisiveness was affecting Mathias as well. His silence. His anger. His pain. They all made sense to me now.

"Then what did you wish to say?"

"It's just that you look, well...you look a little pale. I was worried."

The tight smile that crossed his lips looked more like a grimace and left me aching for the beautiful smile he shared with me the day we met.

"Thank you for your concern, Mairin. I am, however, entirely well. Paleness is a side effect of my...condition, as you well know."

"Oh. Right. Of course it is." I felt like a complete idiot.

"Was there anything else you wished to say to me?"

There were so many things I wanted to say to him, but none of them were healthy for either of us. "I love you" wasn't appropriate for someone you were afraid of. "I miss you" wasn't something you said to someone you had loudly and repeatedly banished from your life.

"Um, no. I guess not."

"Then I will bid you a good afternoon." He was gone before I could return the sentiment.

I drew a deep, shuddering breath and tried desperately to contain the tears that rose to choke me as I watched him stalk to his car. I saw him jerk once as I hitched in another breath, but he kept walking.

"Oh look, the little dyke is crying for the boy she ditched," Stephanie taunted from behind me. I didn't wait to hear what else she might come up with. I ran to the Nova, cranking the engine and the radio to drown out everything but the thundering pace of my heart.

He hated me. It wasn't just that he was keeping his distance because I had asked him to. He truly hated me. I'd shoved him away in the most horrible way possible. I'd denied the very heart of what he was, called it disgusting and hateful and I'd destroyed the only chance at love I'd ever been given.

Kerry and Cecelia found me hunched over my steering wheel, sobbing. I saw them look at each other before apparently deciding to let me get it out of my system before they asked me the obvious question.

"Mathias?" Cecelia asked softly, alternately rubbing my back and patting my shoulder.

I nodded. "He hates me."

"Good," Kerry said. "It's better that way, Maire. You know it is."

I shook my head, letting the pain roll through me and wash away with my tears. I slowly gained control of myself, letting the tears stop on their own rather than forcing them back as I had so often in the last six months. When I was done, I felt better than I had in a very long time.

"Well, it's about time, Maire," Cecelia said, hugging me.

"What's about time."

"You finally cried. I've been waiting for you to cry for six months."

"Oh." I didn't know what to say about that. I'd spent the last six months pretending everything was fine. I didn't cry. I didn't scream. I didn't do much of anything, but pretend to be okay. It was a horrible shock to find out I hadn't fooled anyone but myself.

I dropped Cecelia at her house and drove to The Astral Plane. Kerry was quiet for most of the ride, but spoke up as we looked for parking outside the shop.

"I didn't understand," she said softly.

"What didn't you understand, sis?"

"You love him. Still."

"Yeah, I do."

"I'm sorry I wasn't more supportive," she said.

"It's OK"

"No, it really isn't. I should have known that you wouldn't...couldn't love someone evil. I let Tawnya's fear overrule what I know about you."

She hugged me, something I realized she hadn't done in a long time. "I'm sorry Maire. Can you forgive me?"

I hugged her back, as hard as I could, happy for the contact with another person who loved me. "Nothing to forgive, sis. You were looking out for me. Thanks for caring enough, for loving me enough, to worry about who I love."

Mom was at the shop counter with an older, gray-haired woman when we opened the door. Xavier stood behind the stranger, a tight smile plastered on his lips.

"Oh good, you're here," she said. "I was hoping you wouldn't forget."

Kerry stopped at the door, staring at Xavier. I glanced back and forth between them. Kerry's aura pulsed in time with Xavier's. It was the first time I'd ever seen that happen and I didn't know what to make of it.

"I'm gonna go talk to Tawnya," Kerry said, squeezing my hand before she headed for the reading room at almost a run. She brushed past Xavier and their auras sparked. I filed that away as something to research later.

"Mairin, this is Elise Meyers, the psychic I told you about."

"Pleased to meet you," I said, silently noting her purple aura.

"And this is my grandson, Xavier. He drives me around when I need to leave East Hampton." Elise smiled fondly at Xavier, who flushed.

"Gram, I'm gonna go to the coffee shop. I'll be back in two hours." Xavier kissed his grandmother's cheek before bolting for the door. It was obvious he didn't want to stick around for the psychic lessons and I was glad to see him go. He made me think of Mathias, something I didn't feel up to after my meltdown.

"Elise has agreed to help you work with your new gift," Mom said.

"Your mother tells me that you're able to see auras," Elise said. She sat down on one of the old chintz chairs Mom kept in the shop for clients and waved to another.

"Yeah. At least that's what we think I'm seeing."

"What color aura do you see around me?"

"Purple, kind of dark, and pulsing slightly."

Elise nodded. I saw my mother slip into the back of the shop, leaving me alone with the psychic. She was always open about getting me help with my "gifts," but once the help arrived, Mom bolted. I wondered, sometimes, if she wasn't afraid of me and my "gifts."

"Do you know what my aura tells you about me?" Elise asked.

"No. I know it's the first purple aura I've seen. Most of the auras I see are blue."

"That's to be expected. Blue is the color of human auras."

I jerked back in my seat. What did that make Xavier? "Does that mean..."

"That I'm not human? No. My aura is a combination of the blue aura of a human and the red energy of magic. I'm a witch, Mairin, but still human."

I relaxed slightly, but remained on edge while Elise explained the meaning of the colors I'd seen. I didn't bring up Xavier's orange aura and neither did Elise. It was almost as though she didn't want to have to explain her grandson to me. She was, however, very interested in Braden Lambert's aura.

"Dark, muddy green, you say?" she asked.

"Yeah. It's kind of creepy because it's the only one I've seen like that."

"I should hope so. Green auras are only found around demigods...the children of humans and angels or demons--fallen angels."

I was surprised. "If Braden is the child of an angel, why is he so awful?"

"All of God's creatures have free will, Mairin," Elise said. "It is Braden's choice to be awful, as you say. His aura reflects his choices. If he were a better...person, for lack of a better word...his aura would be clear green. The muddiness tells you that he's chosen his path of 'awfulness.'"

Understanding, as clear as it was horrible, dawned in my heart. "The clarity of someone's aura reflects the clarity of their soul?" I asked, dreading the answer.

"That's certainly one way to look at it."

"So no matter what a person is, if their soul is pure, their aura will be clear?"

"That has been my experience, yes."

"Oh."

Mathias' aura had always been a pale, clear gold, unless he was angry. When his temper got the better of him, as it had when Stephanie had brought up my father's death in the cafeteria so many months ago, his aura darkened and become cloudy. But when he was in control of himself, Mathias' aura was a perfect reflection of the deeply pure soul he possessed.

"All of God's creatures have free will," I repeated Elise's words. "They can choose to be good or evil, in spite of the hand dealt to them."

"Yes."

"Even a vampire can choose to be good, can have a soul so pure his aura is clear gold."

Elise's eyes widened. "A vampire? You've seen this vampire in Highland Home?"

"Yes."

"And he has a clear gold aura, you say?"

"Unless he is angry, yes. When he's angry it darkens."

"Interesting," Elise tapped her fingernail on the arm of her chair. "I've never met a vampire who chose to be good, but in theory it would be possible. It would be excruciating for him much of the time, but it would be possible."

"Why would it be excruciating?" I was afraid I already knew the answer to my question, but I had to know for certain.

"He would have to fight the very real, biological need to feed in order to be around humans and not kill them. From the explanation I've had from vampires, that thirst is extremely painful, especially if the vampire denies it."

Mathias had chosen to be good, chosen to keep the deeply beautiful soul he'd had as a human even when his humanity had been stripped from him on the cobblestones of our harbor in 1922. He had chosen to resist the pain his thirst caused him in order to live in the light among humans for almost a century. And I had rejected him because I thought he wasn't trying hard enough not to kill his food.

The hypocrisy of my rejection hit me like a punch in the gut. Mathias had never once repudiated me because I ate meat someone else killed and sent to a supermarket. My self-righteous indignation felt cold and ugly as I realized there was little difference between the hamburger I ate for lunch and the donors who offered Mathias their blood, save one. Mathias' food volunteered. Mine had no choice.

Chapter 8

The corner of the dimly lit bar was occupied by a young woman. She looked up as Mathias approached. Her smile was wide and inviting and it made my stomach clench with jealousy. Mathias did not return the smile. The deep purple bruises under his eyes made his normally black eyes appear even darker.

"You are willing?" Mathias asked through clenched teeth.

"Extremely."

Mathias sat next to the woman and motioned to the barmaid. She set an empty glass on the table before turning away.

"What's your name, lover?" the woman in the booth whispered.

"Mathias." He took the woman's arm, running his fingers from her wrist to the bend of her elbow.

"Don't you want to know mine?"

"I care only that you are willing," he said. "Have you changed your mind?"

"No. Most other vamps want to talk is all."

"I do not." There was a flash of silver and the girl gasped. Mathias slipped the wine glass under the girl's elbow where it caught the thin stream of blood flowing from the cut he'd made on her inner arm.

The girl's eyes were glassy and she smiled vacantly as Mathias carefully held the tiny blade he'd used to cut her away from himself. He slipped a handkerchief from his pocket and wrapped it over the cut to stop the blood flow. The glass had no more than an inch of blood in it.

"You have my thanks," he said, rising and taking the glass with him. Before he turned away, he dropped several bills on the table. Mathias carefully walked across the bar to an empty booth as far from the woman as he could get and sat alone.

As the dream faded, I saw Mathias lift the glass to his lips. His eyes closed in near ecstasy as his throat worked.

***

My bedroom was dim and distant in the early morning light. My gut was still clenched tight with jealousy for the woman in the bar and it took several minutes for me to process anything more than what that woman had done for Mathias.

When rational thought returned, I was humbled by what I'd seen. That woman had done something so selfless, something I didn't think I could do. And Mathias had left her alive. Not only had he left her alive, he had paid her and been deliberately distant to her. It was only because I'd seen his memories and heard his screams of anguish that I could see the difference between the meal I'd just dreamed of and those that had come before.

The tiny amount of blood Mathias had taken from the woman explained his sickly appearance as well. He was consuming only enough blood to keep himself alive and he was suffering. For me.

I realized it was my disgust with his feeding that had likely prompted the change. Hadn't he told me he'd starve himself if it meant I would stay with him? He wasn't starving, but it was a near thing.

I wanted to believe this dream more than any other dream I'd ever had. Mathias hadn't killed that woman. He had taken what he'd needed, but there had been no frenzy, no death. The whole thing had been rather civilized. I closed my eyes and curled onto my side. For the first time in my life, I sought sleep and the dreams it would bring.

"I love you, Mathias," I whispered and let Morpheus claim me once again.

***

I watched Mathias walk across the parking lot, marveling at the beauty of the clear gold aura that surrounded his beloved face. Though several weeks had passed since Elise had helped me understand the meaning of Mathias' aura, I hadn't devised a plausible reason to speak with him again. I had to admit I was a coward. I couldn't pluck up enough courage to just tell him I'd made a mistake, that I had been horribly wrong about him.

I mean really, how did you walk up to someone and say, "You know, I'm really sorry I freaked out about the fact that you kill what you eat. I see how hypocritical that is when everything I eat has to be killed for me. Can you forgive me and let me love you?" The enormity of what I'd done, the depth of the insult I issued, was such that I just couldn't do it. I couldn't apologize.

Resigned to another depressing day attending classes along side Mathias, but not speaking to him, I stepped out of my car and headed for the school entrance. Kerry had dashed into the school as soon as we'd arrived, leaving me to wait for and silently watch Mathias' arrival alone. Kerry had been great with helping me to convince Tawnya that we'd been wrong about Mathias, but she wouldn't help me fess up to him about my revelation. Tawnya still wasn't convinced Mathias wasn't the most evil creature in Highland Home, but she had stopped cheering when the topic of me not seeing him came up. As for me coming clean with Mathias about my mistake, I was definitely on my own. No one wanted to be the one to say it, but I knew. I'd made the mess and I would have to clean it up. I would have to find a way to redeem myself if I wanted my chance at happiness with Mathias.

Kerry's voice raised in anger snapped me out of my reverie. Students were streaming past me, rushing to the site of what sounded like a barroom brawl. I charged around the corner with the other students, praying I would be in time to save Kerry from whatever was going on. As I rounded the corner, Kerry screamed, "You hateful, spiteful bitch!"

Kerry was squared off with Stephanie Bartlet. The two girls were surrounded by what looked like the entire cheerleading squad and most of the football team.

The Golden Ones screamed and shouted. Someone started to chant, "lesbo," while someone else screamed, "dyke." Braden's aura was nearly black as he gleefully egged Stephanie on.

"Give her hell, honey," he shouted.

I shoved, twisted and pushed until I broke through the circle of spectators and stepped between Kerry and Stephanie.

"Kerry, what are you doing?" I shouted at my sister. "You know this isn't how to handle anything."

"You didn't hear what she said, Maire." Kerry's voice broke and I saw that she was on the verge of tears. "She said you'd wished Daddy dead. That you could have saved him. That you wanted him to die." Tears streamed down my sister's face and my heart ached for her.

"It doesn't matter what she says, Kerr. We know the truth." I hugged Kerry, trying to calm her enough to get her out of the circle and away from Stephanie before someone got hurt. Kerry's temper was volatile at best. I'd seen her get into tousles with bigger kids when she was younger and she'd always come out on top physically. The problems came later when the guilt for having hurt someone struck down my usually quiet and loving sister. I knew if I didn't help her get her temper under control, she'd do something she'd regret later.

"Back off, dyke," Stephanie shouted, shoving me from behind. "If your lesbo little sister wants a fight, she'll get one."

I turned, pushing Kerry behind me. "Stephanie, I've put up with your crap for years. I've ignored the foul things you've said about me and the people I love most in this world. I've walked away rather than fight you, time and time again. What is wrong with you that you can't just give it up?"

Stephanie swaggered across the circle, showing off for the crowd. "What should I give up, dyke? What are you going to do to make me stop anything? You're weak and you have zero power in this school or in this town."

My own temper was rising. "I am not weak, you twit. Do you think a weakling could have put up with your stupid ass for as long as I have? A weakling would have beat the crap out of you years ago."

"So you think you can take me, dyke?"

"You're not worth it, Stephanie. You never have been." I turned back to Kerry and started to lead her out of the way again.

What happened next was a blur that no one could clearly explain later. Cecelia screamed my name. I turned in time to see Stephanie charging across the circle and I pushed Kerry away, hoping she would get clear of the carnage. I held my ground and waited for the screeching cheerleader to hit me. My eyes were closed when I heard the incredibly sweet and deeply terrifying sound of Mathias' growl. The hairs on my neck stood up and my heart thundered as though it were beating for the first time since I'd left Mathias' home in September. He was here, standing between me and my enemy. It didn't matter what his words told me. This action, this one act of protection, showed me the depth of his feelings for me. He was willing to expose himself, to have to leave Highland Home, to keep a stupid teenager from hurting me. I couldn't let that happen.

"Coward," he growled. "You dare to attack when your opponent's back is turned. Have you no honor?"

I opened my eyes and drank in the scene before me. Mathias stood between me and a clearly terrified Stephanie. His back was to me, but he held one hand behind him. I wanted nothing more than to step forward and take his hand, to let him know I was safe and he didn't need to do anything more, but I held back.

"You can't touch me," Stephanie whispered, backing away from Mathias.

"That is what you fervently pray to be true, coward, but do not test your theory today."

"Touch her and die, freak," Braden thundered, stepping into the center of the circle and pushing Stephanie behind his back.

"Would you care to find out which of us would survive, mongrel?" Mathias growled. "I find I am in the mood to battle."

Across the circle, I could see teachers beginning to stream into the hall. This was about to become an ugly scene where adults who had no idea what was really happening would intervene and possibly get hurt. They would have no idea that a demigod with a penchant for hurting people was trying to pick a fight with a vampire who wouldn't hurt anyone unless they tried to hurt me. I couldn't let Mathias get hurt, or allow him to be held responsible for what should have been nothing more than a quick squabble between teenage girls. I took the step that closed the gap between us and put my hand on Mathias' arm.

"Mathias, please," I said softly. "Teachers are on their way. Kerry is fine. I'm fine. Let it go. Please."

He looked down at me, pausing to glance at my hand on his arm before focusing on my face. I let myself drown in his eyes and despite the stress of the situation, I prayed it would continue forever. There was no anger in his gaze, only the love he had once shown me. I watched the darkness drain out of his aura as the hardness returned to his gaze. I shivered under the frigid look he gave me as he stepped away from me.

"As you wish, Mairin," he said. He looked at me for a moment more before he stalked out of the building.

"All right everyone, break it up, break it up." The assistant principal began herding students out of the lobby. Kerry and I blended into the crowd, escaping the scene of the fight without getting pulled into the disciplinary actions. I heard Stephanie crying and Braden swearing Mathias had started the fight.

"She's going to get away with it all, isn't she, Mairin?" Kerry asked.

"She always does. The principal won't punish her and risk the yearly donation the Bartlet Foundation makes to his favorite charity."

"How do you stand it?"

"Practice and patience. That and I know I'll be able to leave Highland Home, go to college, and live a happy life where Stephanie Bartlet can't touch me."

Kerry smiled sadly before heading for her homeroom in the freshman hall. I reached my own homeroom in time for Cecelia to pop out of the room and grab me.

"That was amazing!" Cecelia exclaimed. "Did you see how Mathias just appeared in the middle of all that?"

"Actually, no. I had my eyes closed. I figured that was safer than watching Stephanie throw a punch."

"Wimp," she teased, dragging me into the classroom. "Well, at least you know for sure he doesn't actually hate you. Nobody could be that ferocious in protecting someone they hated."

Cecelia's words tugged at something in my chest. "It doesn't really matter, Cece. He still won't talk to me."

"That's because you're too chicken to tell him what's on your mind. If you don't do it soon, I swear I'm going to tell him for you."

"Tell him what?"

"That you love him and you forgive him for whatever it was that drove you away in the first place."

"I wish it were that simple, Cece. I have a lot more to beg forgiveness for than he ever did."

"I don't believe that, Maire. You're a good person. You always have been." Cecelia flopped into her chair and leaned in as close as she could. "As for Mathias, you obviously love him. What could be more simple than telling him? You're the one making everything so complicated."

Cecelia's words echoed through my brain for the rest of the day. Was I really the one making everything complicated? Could it be a simple matter of cornering Mathias and telling him I loved him?

I imagined going to his home and pounding on the door until he opened it. He would be framed in the lovely entrance way, surrounded by the beautiful home he chosen because he loved the stretch of beach behind it. He would be cold and distant, but I would be firm and insist he listen to me. I would tell him of my love. I would apologize. I would beg his forgiveness and beg that he stay with me. In my dreams, Mathias would sweep me into his arms and kiss me and we would live happily ever after. The daydream was certainly pleasant enough, but unless I was willing to put my heart and happiness on the line and risk his rejection, nothing would change between us. I didn't know if I was strong enough to risk that much, but I knew if I didn't try something, I would regret it for the rest of my life.

I dropped Kerry at the house before I headed to The Astral Plane for another lesson with Elise. As much as I had hated the psychics Mom had found for me to work with on my dreams, I liked Elise. I was learning not only what the auras I saw meant about the people to whom they were attached, but how to help those people heal damaged auras or clear muddied ones. We had had a particularly good session last week where I helped a young woman from East Hampton heal a tear in her aura that had been caused by an encounter with a demon. It terrified me to think that there really were demons walking the earth, but what I was learning was worth every moment of fear.

My only issue with Elise was her grandson. Xavier came with his grandmother every time she came to The Astral Plane. He'd wait with her at the shop until I arrived. Once I was there, he would stare at me, sniff the air as he'd done that night at the football stadium, and then leave. It took weeks for me to figure out Xavier hadn't believed me when I'd sworn I wouldn't let Mathias change me into a vampire. He kept checking to be sure he didn't have a reason to seek out Mathias. I shuddered to think what would happen if Xavier deemed Mathias enough of a threat to go after him.

I pulled into a parking space about two blocks from the shop. Parking after school was always such a hassle. The downtown had gone through one of those revitalizations a few years ago and there were trendy shops like my mom's up and down the three blocks considered "downtown." The coffee shop the Golden Ones favored was overflowing onto the sidewalk. I hurried past it when I noticed Stephanie and Braden holding court in the center of the group of tables the shop had in their courtyard. I didn't want to risk them seeing me, so I ducked down an alley that took me past one of the few historic homes still standing in Highland Home. In the garden behind the beautiful home, a flash of glossy black and shimmering gold caught my eye.

Mathias stood in the garden, his head bowed. Something about how still he was, how tired he looked, stopped me. I slipped quietly up the path, feeling like an intruder, but unable to stop myself.

"Kathryn, would you have been able to forgive what I had become had I not taken your life with my first thirst? Would you have loved me as you always had or would you have run screaming, given the chance? I hope you would have run. I hope you would have lived a long and happy life if our paths had not crossed when they did."

Mathias rubbed his temples. In the bright sunlight, he looked even more pale and tired than he had at school. Something was wrong, though I couldn't imagine what could make a vampire look as tired as Mathias did. I watched as he knelt in the dirt and scooped several handfuls of soil into a glass jar.

"Thank you, my Kathryn," he said, kissing the last handful before dropping it into the jar and screwing the lid on tightly. "My home, my link to the sun. I am ever in your debt." The words had the ring of ritual, but not of the deep emotion Mathias had displayed when he'd told me the tale of Kathryn's death. Something had changed in him, something fundamental.

I ducked behind the house as Mathias rose, thinking he would be walking up the path to the street. Instead, I heard him speaking softly again. I peered around the corner again, tears rising to choke me as I eavesdropped on his deepest thoughts.

"She reminds me of you, Kathryn. Fiery, stubborn, free. She doesn't want my help, doesn't want me to be her knight. So much like you, Kathryn. Would it surprise you to know how she has filled the place in me where you once lived? Would you forgive me? I think you would. You always wanted what was best for others and this girl, this amazing human girl, would be good for me. For her, I would give up the sun. I would live in the darkness if I thought that penance enough to deserve her." Mathias sighed and rubbed his temples again. "I will come back to you, my Kathryn. I must always come home, but I have to leave. I have to give Mairin a chance to be human, to live a life without my disease, without the danger I place her in by being near. I will never be whole without her, but she deserves better. She would hate that I'm doing this for her own good, but I know that as long as I stay here, she will never let go, never move on. I only wish I were deserving of her. If I thought I could redeem myself in her eyes, I would stay with her."

A sob slipped past my lips. Mathias' head jerked up and I turned and ran back to the street, to the swirling mass of humanity that traveled the street unaware of the evil that walked with them. I wondered what color my aura was, how muddy it was for having hurt Mathias so deeply. That he would give up the sun, the one thing he believed kept any part of him human, in penance for the thirst that was beyond his control, was too much for my heart. He thought he didn't deserve me, when in fact I was the one who could never hope to deserve him.

***

Xavier stood outside The Astral Plane, leaning against the wall and watching the street. He pushed away from the wall when he saw me coming.

"Walk with me," he barked and stalked away.

I followed, fear curling in my gut. Xavier had never before looked as he did now. His aura was muddied a bit, and pulsing so much I could physically feel the press of it when I walked beside him.

"The blood sucker went too far today, Mairin," he said. "The pride has decided he has to be taken care of."

"Wait a minute. What the hell are you talking about Xavier? What happened and who the hell is the pride?"

Xavier stopped and threw himself back to lean against the wall of the shop we stood beside. "I didn't tell you all of my story that day I met you at the grocery store. I didn't think you needed to know and when I found out you were going to be working with Gram, I figured you'd bring up my aura and she'd tell you about me."

"I didn't."

"Yeah, I know. You're the strangest girl I've ever met, Mairin. Any other girl would have been all over my Gram with questions. You just let it go." He sighed. "Remember when I told you I didn't choose the job of protector but that I wouldn't back away from it?"

"Yeah."

"You don't choose to be what I am. You get infected. It's a virus and it's incurable."

I shook my head. I still had no idea what he was talking about.

"I was attacked by what my dad thought was a panther on a family trip to Florida when I was kid. Turned out that panther wasn't normal."

I could see Xavier waiting for me to make some connection, but my mind shied away from what he was trying to tell me.

"It was a werepanther," he said finally. "I caught the virus, so now I'm a werepanther too."

"You're kidding," I said before I could stop myself.

"I wish I were. Turns out there were a few other werepanthers in East Hampton. No one knows why we seem to congregate there, but the pride has kind of appointed itself the protectors of the area. We keep the other supernaturals under control. We keep the new wereanimals from infecting others. We keep the passing blood suckers from staying too long or turning anyone. We keep the peace, so to speak."

I couldn't do anything but shake my head. "What the hell is wrong with me?" I asked. "Why am I such a magnet for the impossible?"

"I wondered the same thing actually," Xavier said with a laugh. "Gram says it's because you handle the supernatural well. You don't freak out, so the supernaturals are drawn to you."

"Great. I'm a weird magnet and you think it's funny."

Xavier sobered. "I don't think it's funny, Mairin. I think it's as sad as a seven year old boy being infected with an incurable disease that makes him furry once a month."

"You really turn into a cat once a month?"

"More than once a month if there's danger. That's what I came to talk to you about actually. Mathias openly threatened two humans today. The pride has decided we have to move before he makes good on those threats."

"What do you mean the 'pride has decided to move'?"

"We're going to take him out, Mairin. He's a danger now. We can't let him live."

The breath stopped in my lungs. "No," I whispered. "You don't know what you're saying, Xavier."

"The moment he threatened those kids today, Mairin, he sealed his fate."

"No. Xavier, you can't do this." I grabbed his shoulder to keep from falling. "He's not evil, Xavier. He's not even mean. You know I've talked to Elise about him, his aura. He's one of the purest souls you'll ever meet. To take his life would be...would be a sin!"

"You don't get it, Mairin. There's no choice to be made. He threatened humans. The pride takes that seriously and we are sworn to protect humans over supernaturals."

"Wait, who did he threaten?"

"Braden Lambert and Stephanie Bartlet."

"That's only one human, Xavier and I can tell you that Mathias would never hurt Stephanie."

"What do you mean? What about Braden?"

"Braden isn't human. He's a demigod and an evil one at that. His aura is so clouded by his evil it's almost black. Didn't Elise tell you?"

"No." Xavier considered what I said for a moment. "It doesn't matter. Braden is at least part human. If the blood sucker would hurt him, he must die."

"So you and your pride," I spat the word as though it were as filthy as it felt on my tongue. "have decided that good and evil are determined by species and not nature?"

"It's not that simple, Mairin."

"It sure sounds like it is. I can tell you, in no uncertain terms, that Braden is evil to his core. But according to you, because he's still marginally human, his life is worth more than Mathias'."

"If you want to look at it that way, then yes," Xavier said. His aura was pulsing with anger and I realized I could see the shadowy shape of a cat stalking back and forth amid the orange sparks.

"No, it's not how I look at it, it's how it is. You and your pride, you're all hypocrites. Mathias is the furthest thing from evil in this godforsaken town, but you've condemned him for what he is and what he might do, while Braden has harmed humans, has damn near killed kids on a football field and he lives without your pride threatening to kill him."

"Mairin, I'm not going to argue this with you. The pride has made its decision. I only wanted you to know what was happening so you could stay out of it."

"I won't let you do this. I won't stand by and let you and your pride play God."

"You don't have a choice, Mairin. Just stay out of the way, okay?"

Xavier stalked away, leaving me staring stupidly after him. I couldn't let the pride hurt Mathias. I had to get to him before they did and warn him. I ignored my mother's frantic shouts as I dashed past the shop and headed for my car. The very least I could do was warn Mathias and find a way to get him away from Highland Home before this town became his tomb.

Chapter 9

I pulled into the drive in front of Mathias' home and knew immediately that something was wrong. The shades were drawn in every window. I knew Mathias, who loved the sun more than anything else in his life, would never close up his house like this unless he were leaving. I'd heard him say he was leaving as he'd stood at Kathryn's grave, but I hadn't believed he leave so quickly. He believed leaving would be the best thing he could do for me, but I'd never believed he'd leave without saying goodbye. Despite having come to the house to send Mathias away, my heart sank. I knew I was too late, that he'd already left.

Unwilling to believe he was gone without proof, I banged on the door until my fists were bruised. I walked around the house to the deck outside the kitchen and peered through the glass wall. It was from there that I could see dust covers thrown over furniture. I could feel the emptiness of the house, the missing vibrancy of Mathias' presence. There could be no doubt about it. he was gone.

I sat on the steps of the deck and watched the waves crash onto the beach. The wind whipped past, leaving me chilled, but I couldn't muster the strength to go back to my car to escape the weather. Mathias had left Highland Home. He'd gone without saying goodbye or giving me the chance to beg him to stay. I'd never have the chance to tell him I was sorry, to tell him that I loved him. He was gone and I was numb.

When the sun sank below the horizon and the wind began to truly howl, I left Mathias' house and headed for home. At least Mathias' leaving meant he was no longer in danger from Xavier and his "pride." I may have lost him due to my own hard-headed refusal to own up to my mistakes, but he would live. I could accept that.

"Where have you been?" Mom demanded after I closed the door behind me.

"I had to...I went out to Mathias' house."

"You went where?"

Tawnya's head snapped up.

"I went to Mathias' house, but he's...he's gone. The house is closed up. He probably went back to California."

"He's gone?" Tawnya asked.

I nodded. "Looks like it."

"Good riddance."

I rounded on my mother's partner. "You know what, Tawnya, I'm sick of your attitude toward Mathias. You don't know him. You don't know what he is like. You've made a judgment based on what he is, not who he is. What if everyone did that?"

Mom looked at me as though I had suddenly grown a third eye. The blood drained from Tawnya's face, leaving her pale and shaking. I knew then that Tawnya hadn't shared the truth about herself with my mom. I could see she feared I would expose her secret.

"Mairin, apologize to Tawnya immediately," Mom said.

I shook my head. "I'm sorry for losing my temper, Tawnya, but I'm not sorry for finally speaking my mind."

"It's all right, Loraine," Tawnya said when my mom began to object to my apology. "Mairin is right. I made a judgment of that boy based on something beyond his control and didn't accept Mairin's assessment of him. That was both cruel and unfair."

Tawnya held her hand out to me and I hugged her. Her apology wasn't acceptance of Mathias, but it did make me feel a little better. If an angel could admit she was wrong about a vampire, maybe there was hope for the werepanthers in East Hampton after all.

Shari Richardson | 123

"I wish I knew what was going on with you, Mairin," Mom said, sitting down next to Tawnya. "Help me understand. Help me help you, honey."

I sighed and sat across from them. "I made a huge mistake last September. I let fear rule me rather than believing in myself. I don't think anyone else can help me, Mom. I missed my chance to make things right and I need to move on."

"What did you do, baby?"

"Exactly what I just accused Tawnya of," I said. "I didn't have enough faith in Mathias to trust him to do the right thing and now that I know," I looked hard at Tawnya, "without a doubt that he has changed because he knew I couldn't live with is choices, I've lost him. I'm an idiot."

"You're not an idiot," Mom said. "You're a teenaged girl. You're supposed to be unsure and have doubts. I'm sorry that Mathias is gone, but I'm glad you're coming back to us."

I didn't know that I was going to come back the way my mom wanted me to, but she was right that with Mathias gone, I would have to move forward.

"You've always put everyone else ahead of you, Mairin," Tawnya said. "As much as I may not care for Mathias, I'm glad that you finally saw that there are those outside your family who will put your well being ahead of their own."

I grimaced. Mathias leaving for my own good still stung. "I'm kind of worn out. Is it OK if I go to bed?"

"Of course, sweetie. Are you sure you don't want anything to eat first?"

"No. I just need to get some sleep. I'll see you in the morning."

In my room, I put on my pajamas and curled up on my bed. "I'm so sorry, Mathias," I whispered. "Be happy wherever you've gone to. Live in the sun, my love. My heart, my mourning sun."

***

"She's not here," Mathias said, glancing around the darkened football field.

"Of course not, leech," Braden sneered. "I knew I didn't actually need her to get you here. I figured why make more mess than necessary."

Mathias' deep growl tore from between his lips. He paced under the goal post, his dark hair ruffling in the wind. At the other end of the field, Braden waited.

"What's it going to be, blood sucker?"

Mathias nodded once and stepped on the field. Around him, the night lit up with a dozen bright points of light. Feline eyes followed the movement of both boys, though I could see how they watched Mathias more closely than they did Braden.

"Why have you involved the cats, mongrel?" Mathias asked. "Do you not believe you are the better man in this battle?"

Braden's laugh was a harsh bark. "I don't need any fucking cats to take out one blood sucker. But I don't mind an audience."

Mathias stopped on the fifty yard line and waited for Braden to join him there. "You wanted this battle, mongrel. What are your terms?"

"Well, I suppose to be fair, I should tell you that those cats out there plan to tear out your throat if you get the upper hand on me, but they're willing to let us fight it out before they act."

"Thank you for the warning."

"I guess I also feel kind of bad for that girl of yours especially since I threatened to kidnap her to get you here. I'm willing to get Stephanie to back off if I'm the one who walks off this field tonight. In fact, I'll do one better than that. Steph's a bitch anyway. I'll make sure she leaves your girl and her family alone. I'll protect her, keep her safe until the younger one graduates. But I can't do any of that if I don't win."

"So if I am willing to lay down my life, you will care for Mairin and Kerry?"

"That's the gist of it, blood sucker. This isn't personal. It's business. You're dangerous. You're evil and you've got to go." Braden laughed again. I could see the blackness swirling in his aura. "Well, it's a little personal. I don't like anyone thinking they can take me on without consequence."

"I hope you won't mind if I'm not selfless enough to go without a fight," Mathias said with a small, bitter smile.

"I was hoping you'd say that."

There was a coughing howl from one of the cats. "Oh yeah," Braden said. "If you happen to get lucky and kill me, the cats say they'll make sure your girl is safe."

"After they've finished me off, of course."

"Of course." Braden's smile was gleeful. "I guess I win no matter what."

"It would appear that the deck is stacked in your favor, mongrel, but I find I don't mind the stakes. Shall we begin?"

"Such a gentleman for a blood sucking, soulless monster."

"Perhaps you might consider learning some manners for your next life," Mathias bowed before dropping into a defensive crouch. "Come get me, mongrel. I tire of talking."

The battle raged up and down the length of the football field. The sound of the vampire and the demigod colliding shook the stadium to its foundation. Around the edge of the field, the cats lay waiting. Their luminescent eyes followed the battle closely. Their muscles remained tense as they awaited the moment when they would abandon their vigil or join the fray.

Mathias charged Braden, stumbling as they drew close. Braden seized the advantage, roaring with triumph. The quarterback tackled Mathias, pinning his body to the ground while lifting Mathias' shoulders off the ground. Braden brought his fist back to land the killing blow, the one that would strip Mathias' head from his shoulders.

***

I screamed. Over and over the anguish poured from my throat. I struggled frantically to free myself of the bonds of sleep. I had to get out of the dream so I could go to the football field and stop the insanity. My bedroom door flew open, and Mom flew into the room.

"Mairin, my God, baby, what is it?"

"Mathias," I screamed.

Mom tried to hold me, but I fought her. "Let me go. You have to let me go. I might still have time to save him."

"Mairin, honey, Mathias is gone. You said so yourself."

"No, Mom. He's not gone. I have to go. I have to stop them."

Finally free of the covers, I pushed against Mom until she released me. I was dressed and down the stairs before she knew what I was doing.

"Mairin, it's the middle of the night. Where are you going?"

The Nova roared to life. I shot out of the drive and onto our quiet little street. In my panic, I imagined I could hear the thunderous clash of the vampire and demigod as they battled on the football field two miles away. The Nova's tires squealed as I rounded the corner into the school parking lot. I laid down a wide swath of rubber, slamming the Nova into park and dashing for the stadium entrance.

Chapter 10

As I ran toward the stadium, the air was split by deep snarls and growls. It was like something out of the worst of my childhood nightmares, made even worse by the dream in which I'd already seen what was happening outside my vision. I turned the corner and skidded to a stop at the top of the stadium. Two figures in the dark below me ran at each other, throwing their bodies with no regard for injury. Only one goal was evident. They were going to kill each other or tear down the stadium trying. The boom when Braden and Mathias collided shook the stands and nearly knocked me off my feet.

It seemed to take an eternity for me to reach the field. The booming crashes continued as I ran, seeming to come ever more quickly. As I ran, I prayed. Let me make it there in time. Let them stop before they killed each other. Let Mathias be OK. I was dizzy before I reached the railing at the foot of the stairs. I couldn't get my mind to wrap around the one most important thought. The one thing that kept repeating as I ran. What was I going to do to stop the vampire I loved from being killed by the demigod I hated?

Surrounding the field, I could see the glowing eyes of the werepanthers. I knew Xavier and his pride were waiting to take Mathias' life if he were to get lucky enough to beat Braden. I also knew Mathias intended to lay down his life on this field in return for Braden's promise to protect me and my family. I couldn't let that happen. I couldn't let him fight this battle alone.

Braden roared, drawing my eyes unwillingly to his face. I could see triumph in his eyes as Mathias stumbled. The quarterback tackled Mathias, pinning his body to the ground while lifting Mathias' shoulders off the ground.

"No!" I screamed as Braden brought his fist back to land the killing blow, the one that would strip Mathias' head from his shoulders. The muscles in Braden's shoulders bunched and I saw the flash of glee in his eyes. I knew he had the strength and determination to kill Mathias, but did I have the faith to save him?

I vaulted over the railing at the bottom of the stands and rushed onto the field. I passed one of the werepanthers. The cat growled, but I didn't stop. A sane person would have run screaming from the scene playing out on the football field, but then I'd never been sane when it came to Mathias. My only thought was to stop Braden before he could kill the man I loved.

"Braden, stop," I gasped, leaning into the quarterback's body, blocking the blow he was going to throw. "You can't do this. It's wrong and you know it."

Braden shook his head, his shaggy hair falling into his eyes. "He's evil, Mairin. He has to die." Braden pushed me out of the way.

"Who are you to say who is evil?" I demanded. "You've never been particularly good to anyone I've known. How many kids did you beat up last year? How many players did you watch leave the field on stretchers because you used your strength against them? How many choices have you made that have resulted in the blackening of your soul?"

Braden raised his fist again. His usually muddy green aura was a deep, pulsing black. He grinned, enjoying the carnage he wrecked on others. "Get out of here, Mairin. This is going to get messy."

I looked into Mathias' deep, black eyes and saw resignation in them. He was ready to die because he believed his death would save me. I knew Braden wouldn't protect me or Kerry. I knew the moment Mathias was gone, the Golden Ones would resume their abuse of me and my family. I couldn't let Mathias give up his life. I certainly couldn't let him die thinking I couldn't accept what he was. He was a vampire. He killed to live, but then so did every other being on the planet, including me. He was a vampire, but he was also the most deeply compassionate person I had ever met. Mathias' lips curled in the tiniest of smiles and I knew I couldn't let Braden end this magnificent boy's life.

As Braden brought his fist down, I threw myself at him. The shock of my sudden attack altered the direction of the deadly blow, but not the force of it. Bright star bursts flooded my vision and I felt at least one rib crack before I could do nothing but gasp for breath. Painfully, I rolled away from Braden, who leaped to his feet, snarling. He charged and I braced myself for the bone crushing pain I knew was coming.

"No," Mathias roared, jumping up and throwing himself between Braden and me. He crouched over me and used his body to absorb the force of Braden's attack. Mathias lifted Braden, throwing him to the side. The snarling demigod rolled away from us.

"Mairin, my love," Mathias whispered. "Why didn't you let him finish the job? I was ready to leave this existence if you didn't want me. Do you want me to suffer an eternity without you?"

I cupped Mathias' face with my palm, shocked as I always was by the vibrant feel of him beneath my fingers. The months of separation hadn't dimmed the wonderful electrical current that always jumped between us. "I don't want you to suffer," I said. The pain in my chest bloomed bright and hot as I dragged in a breath to tell him the rest. He needed to know I'd decided. I loved him no matter what he was, no matter how he survived. I loved him because of who he was. I tried to speak, but the pain drowned my words in quicksand. Braden's blow had done more than break my ribs.

Mathias' eyes lit with something I had never seen in them before. Always before, Mathias had looked at me with a reserved kind of resignation, as though everything that happened between us did so because it was his fate to live in pain. Now, however, the resignation was gone. In it's place was hope. That hope bloomed for an instant before being replaced with the wary look I hated most. I had wounded him so deeply that he didn't trust his own judgment. He was afraid to hope. That fear was worse than any physical pain I was in.

"Get away from her, leech," Braden growled rising from where Mathias had thrown him.

Mathias turned, crouching protectively over me. "Back off mongrel."

"I will if you will," Braden said with a nasty sneer.

"This will not end well, half-breed," Mathias said. "I have a reason to live now."

"Then I'll take that too," Braden said.

It took several seconds for Braden's threat to sink into my pain-numbed brain, but Mathias got there before me and he wasn't the only one. Behind us, the coughing growl of the werepanthers grew until I could feel the sound vibrating in my chest. Xavier's pride was getting a first hand lesson in the free will of all God's creatures. The more human combatant the pride had backed had just broken their cardinal rule. He'd threatened a human, and a helpless, injured one at that. Mathias was no longer the pride's only target on this battle field.

The ripping growl that slipped between Mathias' lips was alien, something dredged up from the most primordial pits of fear. I closed my eyes to block out the vision of Mathias' beloved face and its link to that growl. I lay cold and shivering in the pale moonlight, searching for the strength to stop Mathias before he did something he would regret.

"Mathias, no," I whispered. I lay my hand on his arm as I had done this morning. Could it really only have been fewer than twenty four hours before when I'd been able to stop him so easily? Now, the stakes were raised and my weak pleading had no affect on him. Moving so quickly I could barely see him, Mathias left my side and grabbed Braden from behind.

"Do you truly wish to finish this, mongrel?" The soft silken tones of Mathias' voice were terrifyingly altered in his anger. The hair on my neck rose, tremors coursed down my spine, wrenching a scream from my lips. I saw Mathias' eyes flick toward me.

"Mathias, please don't," I couldn't put any more voice to my words than a bare whisper but I knew he could hear me.

"He would kill us both, Mairin." Mathias bared his teeth, leaning into Braden's neck.

"No."

Braden's eyes bulged in fear. He'd heard his death in the silky voice behind his ear. The quarterback's face suffused with blood and he pleaded with me silently. I couldn't let Mathias sacrifice anymore of his soul to this horrible boy. Behind Braden, Mathias' eyes were narrowed, his teeth bared. Strangely I did not fear Mathias, not even as he considered murdering Braden in front of me. My only thought was of protecting him from damaging his soul.

"No," I whispered again. "Don't let him take anything more from you."

Mathias roared in frustration. His jaw worked and I could see the thirst rise in his eyes. Braden had become prey and Mathias was a predator of such danger and efficiency that he could finish the burly quarterback without breaking a sweat or pausing for a moment's remorse.

"Why does it matter what kind of monster I am?" Mathias demanded. "I'm a monster in your eyes, nothing else matters."

I shook my head, struggling to breathe past the pain in my chest that had nothing to do with my broken ribs. "Not a monster," I whispered. "Never a monster."

Mathias flung Braden's body away. He stood for a moment, staring at his hands in disgust before he knelt beside me.

"What has changed, Mairin?" he asked. "What does it matter if I kill? You cannot love me and I do not wish to live without you...without your love. I thought I could leave you, but I didn't even make it out of Highland Home before I returned to find you at my home. I might have tried to leave again if the mongrel hadn't called to tell me he'd taken you after you'd left the house."

Xavier stepped out of the shadows and answered Mathias. "It does matter, leech," he said. "If you can choose to not kill, you might be worth saving."

Mathias stared blankly Xavier, who nodded once to the cats around the field. They closed in on Braden, surrounding the kneeling quarterback.

"You proved us wrong tonight," Xavier said to Braden. "Always we have taken the side of humans and part human creatures over wholly supernatural beings. Mairin told me we were wrong, but I didn't believe her until now. We'll be watching you, demigod." He turned back to Mathias. "Maybe this crappy little town might be more interesting if we keep you around, but remember, we'll be watching you."

Xavier slipped a cell phone from his pocket and dialed 911. The siren rose and fell in the darkness outside the football stadium, shrieking like a banshee.

"Better figure out what you're going to tell the paramedics when they get here," he said. "I'm thinking she tripped over the railing."

I nodded, shrieking when the movement ground the ends of my broken ribs together.

"Another time, then, kitty," Mathias growled, smiling broadly.

"Anytime, leech," Xavier agreed.

"You're both nuts," I whispered. The darkness claimed me then, leaving me to wonder if the vampire and the werepanther could refrain from killing each other while we waited for the paramedics.

***

My mom and Tawnya met us at the hospital. I could see from the way they watched Mathias that I'd have a ton of questions to answer when I was feeling better. Tawnya may have admitted that she'd been wrong about Mathias, but that had been when she was safe to say so, when Mathias had been gone from Highland Home. Now that she saw he hadn't left, I was sure she'd give me problems about him. I'd have to deal with that problem when it came to a head. For now, I focused on breathing.

"Mairin, you scared me to death tonight. You are never to do anything like that again. What possessed you to go tearing out of our house in the middle of the night?" Mom tried to hug me, but couldn't find a way to get close to me through the hospital equipment.

"Dream," was all I could whisper. I knew she wouldn't ask any more questions once she understood a dream had sent me into the night looking to help someone. I was right. She nodded once and continued to watch Mathias as the doctors worked around me.

Mathias stood back, watching the doctors work. I saw his eyes widen just once as the doctor set an IV into my arm. The flash of blood in the line was gone quickly, but Mathias had see it and so had I.

"Do you need to go?" I whispered.

He smiled and shook his head. "If you'll have me, I will stay."

When I was strapped, taped and bandaged to within an inch of my life, the doctor told everyone to get out.

Mathias laid his hand in mine and I grasped it frantically. "Don't go," I pleaded. "Not yet."

Mathias turned to the doctor who must have seen something desperate enough in my face to change his mind.

"Five minutes," the doctor said, leaving me alone with Mathias and my family.

"Mom, I need to talk to Mathias. Alone."

"I'll be right outside," she said. She kissed my forehead and pulled Tawnya from the room.

Mathias waited until the door closed behind them before gently pulling his hand from my grasp. I tried to recapture it, but he held himself away from me. My heart ached even more deeply than my broken ribs.

"Mathias, I need you to understand," I said.

"There is nothing to understand, Mairin," he said. I could see the cold edge creeping into his eyes. "You made yourself quite clear. I only wonder why you came to the field. You should have let that mongrel finish me."

"Never," I said. "Do you want me to suffer an eternity without you?" Mathias jerked as I turned his words back to him.

He closed the space between us quickly. My heart thundered in my chest, the natural beats echoed by the monitor beeping next to the bed. "Why do you continue to taunt me like this?" he asked. "There is nothing else to be said."

"But there is," I said.

"What else do you want to say, Mairin? Do you want to be more specific about the ways in which you loathe me? Do you need me to know that your family will be joining with the cats in watching me and my murderous ways?" Bitterness made his words hard and painful. "What else can you possibly need to say to me?" he demanded.

"I love you," I said.

"None of if matters, of course, because I'll be gone before morning. I would have been long gone if that mongrel hadn't threatened you....What did you say?"

"I love you."

Mathias blinked slowly. "You love me?"

I nodded, grimacing when the pain snatched at my chest.

"And when did you come to this conclusion?" he asked. He was wary and hesitant, but I saw a flash of the hope I'd seen in his eyes on the football field.

"About three minutes after you appeared in my life," I said. "I'm only sorry I was too much of a coward to tell you sooner."

The muscles in his neck clenched and I could tell he was gritting his teeth. "You love me," he said softly.

"Yes."

"No matter what. No matter that I am killer, that I have killed even those who were precious to me in my quest to sate my thirst."

"No matter what," I said. "I can't keep condemning you for doing what I don't have the courage to do for myself. I let others kill so I can eat. I eat food that doesn't volunteer to be my meal. You care enough about your meals to personally see to them, to wait for them to volunteer before you seek to make them food. I want you to live, Mathias. I'm just hoping you can find a way to be okay with what you have to do to live. The guilt isn't good for either of us."

"You are impossibly silly, Mairin," he said fondly, holding up a hand to stop my protest. "And impossible to resist. Would it surprise you to know I'd already made those decisions before that mongrel came for me? That I have been trying to live without death so that I could deserve you? That is why I've been so pale of late. I've been feeding less, being more careful and leaving my donors alive." He took my hand and held it to his cheek. "I find that I am willing to do whatever I can to stay with you."

"I dreamed you had, but I was afraid to hope. I just knew it didn't matter any more. All that matters is that I can't live without you."

"You dreamed of me feeding?"

I nodded. "The girl in the bar. I wanted that dream to be the truth, but I was afraid to ask."

"What else have you dreamed, Mairin?" His eyes were wary.

"Everything. I've seen you hunt. I've seen you mourn your victims. I..." I didn't know how to tell him I'd seen Kathryn die.

"You saw me rise, didn't you."

"Yes."

"And yet you still love me."

"Yes."

"Why?" His face was a mask of anguish.

"Because you are my sun. You are the light of my life and you are the voice that calls me from my dreams."

Mathias leaned down and I slipped my hand behind his head and pulled his face close to mine. I brushed my lips over his, feeling him clamp them tightly. Always he was afraid I would be infected if he gave in and kissed me, but I had to taste his lips, to seal our love.

"I love you because I know what you are," I said. "You are decent and good and you are the man I love."

Mathias groaned, still refusing to open his lips until he turned from my lips to brush his against my neck. Goosebumps rose along the path his lips took down my neck to my shoulder.

"I don't deserve you," he whispered. "But I want you."

"Time is up, young man," the doctor said, stepping close to my bed and hanging a new IV bag above me.

"Of course," Mathias said, kissing my hand before stepping away from me.

"Don't go," I begged, knowing I meant more than leaving the room.

"Never," he said. "Never again."

Made in the USA
Charleston, SC
03 April 2011